THE STEWARDESS'S DIARY - PART SEVEN

FRANCE

S.M. PRATT

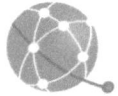

The Stewardess's Diary - Part Seven: France
Copyright © 2017 by S.M. Pratt

Last updated January 25th, 2020
Editing by Samantha Marie

ISBN: 978-1-988639-00-0 (e-book)

ISBN: 978-1-988639-26-0 (paperback)

PROLOGUE

I'M CHARLIE, a veteran pilot for a major international airline that shall remain nameless for reasons you'll soon come to understand.

A year ago, while waiting for my flight to London in the airline's lounge at one of America's largest hubs, I discovered a special and highly personal journal among my belongings. How it happened, I'll never know, but the beautiful brown leather notebook nonetheless appeared in my briefcase at some point between the time I left my New York penthouse apartment and arrived at the airport lounge.

Perhaps it was a mix-up at security, or some devious stewardess with sly hand skills, but I've since become obsessed with the person who wrote that diary, her stories, and—to be blunt—her unconventional sex life.

My best friend—let's call him Bob—is one of my regular co-pilots. Bob advised me to forget about the journal and ignore my hunch to track down its rightful owner. After my initial reading of her hand-written accounts, the part of me who's loyal to the airline and wants the best for our passengers certainly needed to find that stewardess and expel her from our company—or whatever airline she's with. This woman is surely a threat to any crew with her irreverent disregard for our uniforms, her sexual behavior with passengers and airline employees, and the way she ignores regulations. She should clearly be punished for her conduct...

But after reading and re-reading each one of her journal entries, another, more animal part of me has grown fond of her complete lack of boundaries, her willingness to experiment, and her ravenous sexual appetite.

I've had my fair share of illicit affairs with female flight attendants and co-pilots, but none of them were interesting enough to be granted a second fuck by yours truly, let alone be courted or considered for a long-term relationship. But the woman who's filled so many pages with delicate calligraphy and salacious words deserves my full attention. She's certainly maintained it well past the time I closed the cover of her journal—again and again.

Imagining how her naiveté was gradually—and most willingly—robbed from her was simply... enthralling. She's been haunting my wet dreams.

Now, every time I see an unknown stewardess, I wonder if *she*'s the one.

After many conversations with Bob over the past months during our overseas flights, I've come to share some of her journal entries with him. He agrees that I need to locate her. If not for the airline's sake or to satisfy my personal curiosity, then for the mere reason that I could stop obsessing about her and resume paying attention to my actual job: piloting giant aircrafts and safely getting passengers from point A to point B.

The following short stories record my obsession toward her. There are ten in total. Each installment contains my mystery stewardess's original journal entries for a specific location, followed by my own experiences in trying to track her down. You'll discover what (and whom) I did in an effort to identify and locate my stewardess based on the clues she's left in her diary. You can read the episodes in any order, but they'll probably make more sense if you start from the beginning and follow along as I attempt to find her.

And, just to be clear, these stories should *not* land in the hands of any prude or underage person. Some are just romantic, sensual, or highly erotic, while others are immoral, perverse, and possibly even illegal in some parts of the world.

Ah, the things I'll do to this mystery stewardess when I finally encounter her in the flesh!

I'm hard just thinking about it...

Yours truly,

Capt. Charlie
Undisclosed Airline

PART ONE

THE STEWARDESS'S ENTRIES

6:03 A.M.

I WAS LYING CURLED up in the middle of my queen-sized bed, lost in my own fantasy, when a buzz reached my ear.

Go away.

I grabbed my spare pillow and squashed it on top of my exposed ear to muffle the annoying rhythmic noise, but it persisted and pierced my sleepy veil.

Opening my eyes, I looked at the alarm clock on my nightstand: 6:03 a.m.

Who calls this freaking early?

I stretched out for my phone; the number had too many digits to be local. *What the heck?* I cleared my throat in a moot attempt to sound semi-awake. "Hello?"

"*Bonjour, mademoiselle. Je suis Maître Lancelot, le notaire en charge de la succession de Mademoiselle Gabriella Andrews.*"

"What?" I sat up in bed and rubbed my eyes.

Why would some French lawyer call me to talk about my aunt's succession?

"I am sorry. My file says you speak French. We can continue in English."

"I do. Either language is fine. It's just that... it's early here... Are you telling me my aunt Gabriella's dead?"

The line went silent.

"Hello? Are you still there?" I asked.

"I'm so sorry for your loss, miss. I thought you knew. I did not mean to announce such bad news to you in that awful manner."

Now it makes sense... The numerous missed calls from my mom. The email asking me to call her as soon as possible...

"It's alright," I said. "I wasn't very close to her. Barely knew her really."

"Well, it seems she liked you very much because she's left you her French property and business."

"What? Is this a joke?"

"I'm not known for having a sense of humor. So, no. *Mademoiselle* Gabriella's business was quite... particular, and I was calling to see if you could travel to Paris in the near future so I can show it to you. Then you could decide whether or not you want it, or if I should give it to the second person in line."

"Would that be my mother?"

"I'm afraid not. Your mother will be receiving a check for her share of *Mademoiselle* Gabriella's inheritance."

"Can't you just send me a check as well?" The idea of receiving money—whatever the amount— sure sounded good.

"I'm afraid I cannot discuss this matter over the phone. We need to meet in person."

"Is my mother expected to go to Paris as well?" I asked, trying to wrap my head around my schedule, but nothing came to mind. I got up and walked over to my daily planner.

"No, and this phone conversation as well as our upcoming meeting need to remain a secret. *Mademoiselle* Gabriella specifically requested that you be the only person to know about her business. Her sister, your mother, is in no way to be made aware of it. Under no circumstances. Do I make myself clear?"

As if I could tell her anything based on what he's told me...

"Well, I've got a few free days at the end of next week. Would that work for you?" I asked, my fingers tapping on my agenda.

"*Oui, bien sûr.* I'll let you make flight and accommodation arrangements, then please inform me of your date of arrival so I can clear my schedule and meet with you."

"Give me a second," I said while reaching out for a pen. I hated trying to add a new contact to my phone while talking on it.

I wrote his number down, then hung up after he once again shared his condolences for my loss.

Holy shit. What a way to start the freaking day!

6:40 A.M.

NOW WIDE AWAKE, I made a mental note to return my mother's calls. She probably needed a few words of comfort. *Her only sister...* I looked at the clock. *Too early to call her now.*

I headed to the shower and reflected on what I'd just learned while the water droplets massaged my back.

I wasn't particularly close to Gabriella—I hadn't seen her or spoken to her in at least two or three months.

How did she die? Was she sick? Or the victim of a freak accident? Why did she choose me as the one to inherit her business?

Gabriella never married, at least as far as I

knew. She didn't have children of her own, but why not give her business to my mother?

Come to think of it, I don't even know what she did for a living.

I racked my brain while lathering my body with jasmine-scented soap.

I'd last seen Gabriella in a fancy restaurant somewhere in New York City.

What was the occasion? I couldn't recall.

She always dressed in the latest trends. She incarnated modern-day fashion, except for her retro, super long and narrow cigarette holder she always had at the ready... Well as soon as she was outside restaurants and other non-smoking areas.

Maybe she worked in the fashion industry?

She had an air of superiority, but that could have been from her decade-long French immersion. Her cigarette holder didn't help with that either. *Who still used those nowadays?* But it fit with her Audrey Hepburn wannabe look. She'd picked up the typical *Parisian Pretentiousness* syndrome, as I liked to call it. Not every Parisian had it, but I'd encountered enough throughout the years to start naming it.

But, if I have to travel across the globe to deal with this, Paris is probably a good place to do it.

Hair washed, skin exfoliated and squeaky clean, I got out of the shower, patted myself dry, and wrapped my hair in a towel turban before heading to my computer to plan my upcoming trip.

Twenty minutes later, I had booked my flight and hotel. I'd spend three days in the City of Lights. Too bad I couldn't think of a boy-toy to bring along with me. Paris was so romantic. But maybe I could hang out with some old friends I knew who had settled there?

Who is it again? Renée and Luc? And there's also Mark and... what's-her-name?

I decided to check Facebook to see if they were still there. And if so, maybe they'd be around next week?

After some online-stalking and catching up on these friends' lives (at least the parts they shared publicly), I learned that Mark had left town, but Renée was still there. I sent her a private message. Seemed she and Luc no longer were an item (at least based on her relationship status... and he was nowhere to be found on her pictures).

Too bad.

I hated breakups. I loathed having to choose sides. *But do I really have to? Luc was a nice guy. Maybe I should find out what he's been up to?*

I finally found his profile, then saw the photo of someone I hadn't expected to see. Right there, near the top of Luc's timeline, was a post by the man who'd broken my heart over a decade ago. The post, which had 255 likes, announced his upcoming wedding in Paris. I swear my heart winced in my chest. Or maybe it was left-over heartburn from last-night's extra spicy pizza.

Ady... My beloved Ady...

I had cut ties with him long ago. Actually, *he* had cut ties with *me*.

Before Facebook existed, he'd broken up with me via email—what would be a jerky move nowadays—but his work had him gone for months, unable to access phones, so email was probably better than waiting to do it in person.

But obviously, I hadn't become friends with him online—that would have brought on too many painful memories—but it seemed our common friends from back in the day had connected with him on the social platform and were sharing and spreading his good news, and, of course, congratulating him.

I pushed that new information past the precipice of my consciousness.

At least, I tried to.

SO HERE I WAS NOW, a week after learning the bad news, looking out my porthole and mindlessly watching the ground crew wrap up their tasks: bags were being loaded and food resupplied; around me, the voices of friendly flight attendants helped people board and stow their bags.

Not working the flight had left me with nothing better to do than be lost in my own thoughts about my impending sweet-and-sour trip to Paris.

Having to deal with my estranged aunt's inheritance didn't make me happy, but I could use a little extra money, and inheriting a business would surely involve a little of that, right?

The past few days had flown by. I talked to my

mom, to try and console her, but there wasn't much I could do. I tried to learn more about my mysterious aunt, but my mom didn't know much about her own sister either.

I did find myself thinking of my ex, though. A lot. After all those years...

What is wrong with me? Am I afraid of running into him with his new bride while in Paris?

I didn't know the date of their wedding, and I'd been hard on myself, shutting down my computer or phone every time the thought of looking him up arose. I didn't even want to write anything in my journal, afraid it would stir up even more damaging emotions.

The odds of somehow encountering them are slim, especially since I don't know where or when they'll tie the knot.

The stabbing sensation reappeared in my chest again as I buckled up.

What am I really afraid of?

Was it that I could still love him and that seeing him in the flesh would bring up the pain I had somehow managed to put behind me after all those years? Was I afraid that my heart would implode from too much unrequited love?

Then again, maybe one glance at him would be

enough to know that my lips no longer craved his, that my heart no longer longed to be his, and that my pussy no longer craved his cock.

He had quite a good one, though... If I recall.

As the plane finally taxied to the runway for takeoff, I realized that pinpointing the root of my fears was hard, but ignoring them was much, much harder.

So I let my emotions fill my heart with angst and negativity just as the plane's powerful acceleration pushed me into my seat.

THE PLANE RIDE didn't do much to cheer me up.

The woman sitting next to me appeared to be around my age, but dressed to the nines, and with makeup thick enough to completely hide her true skin color.

About ten minutes into the flight, she interrupted the twirling negativity of my inner chatter.

"Can't believe we'll land in Paris tomorrow morning. I'm so excited!" she said.

I politely smiled and nodded, careful not to say anything that could indicate I wanted to chat with her.

"I'm going to visit my oldest daughter. I haven't seen her in nearly a year!"

Guess she isn't a great mind reader. "That's nice," I said with a fake smile.

"Don't think I've ever been this excited in my life... Not recently anyways. Too bad my husband couldn't fly with me today," she said while bringing up the large purse she'd stored below the seat in front of her.

Making small talk with passengers while working is one thing, but don't I deserve the right to enjoy a plane ride in silence when riding as a passenger?

"He couldn't?" I asked, feigning interest forced upon me by my inner courteous self.

"No, he had a deadline to meet. His boss wouldn't let him leave the country before his documents had been handed in. But he told me he was nearly done. A couple of days max. Then he'll be able to join me and our daughter. This is SO exciting!"

I smiled at her, then turned my attention to the buttons on my armrest.

If this woman intends on keeping up her undue exuberance for any extended period, alcohol will certainly help in making her more bearable and less annoying.

I pressed the service button then returned my

attention to the woman, unsure if she was done with her overly happy jabber.

She was now digging through her purse. She pulled a small paperback from it before returning the bag to its temporary home at her feet.

Great! She won't be able to talk while reading, right?

Then I saw the cheesy cover of a bare-chested man with an oiled-up six pack and a few tattoos.

Argh. One of those impossible happily-ever-after romance novels.

God, did I hate how unrealistic their endings were. Then again... Once in my life, I did enjoy those books. But the only true happy endings I'd ever gotten had been purely physical. Real-life relationships that made both people happy didn't exist. I'd long looked for one, but I had since seen the light.

Damn it, girl. Why are you so freaking annoyed by this woman and her choice in books right now? Is my period about to start?

But no calendar check was required. My heart screamed that it was all related to Ady's upcoming wedding. Did a tiny part of me still long for him, my one perfect guy?

Unfortunately, I forgot to look away from her book while lost in my thoughts.

"This book is amazing. Have you read it?" she asked, her light brown eyes meeting mine when I finally looked away from the cover.

I put on the largest fake smile I could muster and shook my head. "Can't say that I have..."

"I highly recommend it. SO hot! Can't put it down!"

The flight attendant reached my seat and depressed my service button. "What can I help you with?" she asked.

"Glass of white wine, please."

"Of course," she said before walking away toward the back of the plane.

I grabbed my headset from the seat pocket in front of me and plugged it in, hoping that my behavior would clue the woman in.

"So why are you going to Paris?" she asked just as I was putting the first earbud in.

I turned to face her. "Someone died."

Her smile dropped. I looked at the screen in front of me and donned my other earbud while my other hand touched the screen.

Good. I should have mentioned it earlier.

Now, what non-romantic movie can I watch?

I PATIENTLY WAITED FOR RENÉE, who had agreed to meet me for dinner on my first evening out in Paris. She'd sent me a Facebook message to say she was running late.

While I sipped my glass of wine, the fashionably-dressed French patrons around me in the bistro offered a good distraction (and so did the few young, loud-mouthed Americans who were enjoying inexpensive local wines).

I let out a yawn.

Jet-lagged, my body wasn't ready for bedtime, but my mind was totally dead from all its mental and emotional juggling over the past week. The afternoon nap I'd taken earlier today didn't help in resetting my internal clock.

And then, just as I blinked away my tiredness, I saw Renée.

My friend was as gorgeous as ever. Highlighted shades of browns and blondes cascaded from the top of her head in a decadent chignon. She wore capri pants and a light blouse, topped by a bright scarf that had too many colors to count. She didn't appear to have any makeup on, save for a smear of peach on her lips. She opened her arms wide and let out a small yelp when she saw me.

I stood up and then closed the gap between us before diving into her open embrace.

"Can't believe it's been so long... It's soooo good to see you!" she said as she held me tight against her Chanel-No.5-scented chest.

"So happy to see you, too!" I said before pulling away. "Come. Sit with me and let's catch up over wine, like in the good ole days."

She smiled at me and nodded, then I turned around and returned to my seat.

A waiter appeared out of nowhere to help my friend take a seat at our table.

"So, how have you been? We have so much to

catch up on... It's been way too long," I said, shaking my head.

She inhaled loudly, then tilted her head while draping the white napkin over her lap. "Life's had its ups and downs. Luc and I broke up. But work has been fantastic."

Talk about getting the Cliff's Notes!

The waiter lifted my already broached bottle of *Le Duc de Belmont* from the table. It was a tasty and inexpensive *Coteaux Bourguignons* vintage he'd recommended about thirty minutes earlier when I'd arrived. He looked at my friend and asked her, "*Un verre de vin, mademoiselle?*"

"*Oui, s'il vous plaît. Merci.*"

I waited until he was done pouring and left us alone before continuing. "Well, that sucks. But let's first toast and then you can tell me all about it—or not—whatever. What do you say?"

She raised her glass and smiled. "To old friends!"

"To old friends," I repeated. "And may we not lose touch for so long again."

We clinked and had a sip.

How amazing were those inexpensive French wines? Even with the bistro markups, they were still very affordable. Once the rich, fruity sip had left my mouth, I returned to the conversation where we'd left it. "I'm so sorry to hear about you and Luc. No chance of getting back with him?"

Renée was downing her glass like she hadn't drunk anything in days. She quickly placed her glass down, empty. She reached for the bottle to refill it before replying to me.

"Once a cheater, always a cheater. No chance in hell."

I was taken aback and almost choked on my current sip. "Luc? A cheater? I would have never guessed."

"Me neither... but I caught him red-handed with the young neighbor, in our bed."

"Well, good riddance, then," I said as I lifted my glass to clink it against hers, hoping her current glassful wouldn't have the same fate as the previous, or else I'd be dragging my friend out on all fours very shortly.

She chuckled then repeated, "Good riddance."

A sigh of relief inadvertently left my lips when she put her glass down after one sip. I tried to cover it up with another question. "Are you dating someone else?"

"No, it's hard to find men now. I mean men

who are interesting enough to have a long-term relationship with."

I smiled in agreement. "I know what you mean. I've given up on that."

She frowned while taking another sip. Once her glass returned to the table, she asked, "What do you mean? Are you into women now?"

I shook my head at my friend. *If only she knew... But I doubt she'd understand.* "I've given up on trying to find 'the one'."

She shrugged. "Don't think I could give up on that." She raised her glass and emptied it again. "And what about your Ady's upcoming wedding? How do you feel about that?"

"I haven't seen him or spoken to him in over a decade."

"Wasn't he 'your one' though?"

"Hard to be someone's 'one' when he doesn't love you back. I guess I was just a fun pastime for him. Nothing more than a two-year hobby... or something like that. My love for him was... inconsequential."

"So, him getting married is not bothering you?"

My heart stung in my chest, but I lied through my teeth. "Guess not." I waved at the waiter and got his attention before pointing to the empty bottle of wine on our table. He circled his finger in the air while his lips seemed to silently voice "*Une autre?*" I nodded. If we were going to be talking about him, I'd definitely need more alcohol in my system.

"Then you won't mind being my plus one at the wedding?"

"What?" I turned to stare at my friend.

"Hey! You said it didn't bother you. Prove it. Plus, I've RSVP'd with plus one and I haven't found anyone to accompany me to the event."

"I'm just here for a few days. I'll likely be gone by then."

"Are you here tomorrow?"

"He's getting married tomorrow?"

"Yep."

I took a long sip, drinking the rest of my glass to appease my competitive side. I couldn't tell my old friend the truth and admit my emotional weakness. I just had to come up with an excuse instead. "But I have a meeting with my aunt's succession lawyer."

"What time?" she asked without losing a beat.

"At 10 a.m."

"That's fine, the ceremony is at 4 p.m. And then the reception is at a hotel right after that."

"Who gets married at 4 p.m. on a Friday?"

"Technically, they're already married. Got

married in the UK a couple of weeks ago. They're just doing a ceremonial wedding here by Notre-Dame, where they met."

I pushed back the pain that was growing in my chest.

Is this jealousy? Or just the cheesy romantic gesture? But, most importantly, can't I talk my way out of this?

"But I don't have an evening gown, or anything fancy to wear." I finally said in a last attempt to be excused from that ceremony.

"Are you kidding me? We're in Paris. There are loads of shops with beautiful dresses. That's not an excuse. More like a good reason to pick up a nice dress and bring it home."

Fuck.

I inhaled deeply, then shook my head. "Then you're coming with me either early tomorrow morning or right after my meeting, and you'll have to help me find something to wear. And help me do up my hair, too!"

"PLEASE, *MADEMOISELLE*. COME IN," said a tall, bald man in a light-gray linen suit.

His shirt was bright blue with white cuffs and collar. Fashion at its finest, and it brought out his matching blue eyes. Even if it weren't for his good looks, his outfit alone would have given any man a three-point hotness bonus. Eleven out of ten.

Not bad for a bald French guy.

"*Croissant? Café?*" he offered after inviting me to sit on the empty chair in front of his massive desk.

"Black coffee would be wonderful, *Maître Lancelot*," I said while taking a seat in the leather chair.

"Please, call me Nicholas," he said with a smile too white to be that of a smoker.

The chair's breadth left plenty of room for me to rest my purse against my hip. I felt tiny compared to everything in his office. His desk had to be eight-feet wide, covered with piles of papers and a very large computer monitor. The glass-paned balcony doors that lined an entire wall had to be twelve-feet high. One of the oil paintings that decorated the other walls was big enough to cover my largest wall back in my apartment.

"Very nice office," I said, forcefully pushing down my stress about the upcoming events. In a weird way, I was grateful for the distraction Gabriella's inheritance was causing... Then again, if she hadn't died, I wouldn't be here in the first place. I would have never heard news related to Ady. He would have stayed in my mental oubliettes where he belonged, along with the painful memories that had swum back to the surface.

"*Oui, merci*," Nicholas said as he handed me a cup of espresso on a tiny saucer. "I like it."

He took a hold of the other cup and saucer, then headed behind his massive cherry desk.

I waited until he was comfortably seated before talking. "So... Now that I've flown all the way to

Paris, will you tell me what this mystery business is all about?"

"Of course." He brought his cup to his lips. After two brief sips, he put it down then exhaled loudly. "I'll tell you everything you want to know, but it's simply not something we could have discussed over the phone."

In one gulp, I emptied my drink then placed the empty cup on his desk, between two tall stacks of important-looking papers. "Enough of the mystery, please. I'm here now, so what is it?"

He straightened his back before aiming his blue eyes at me. "Your aunt—may she rest in peace— ran a very successful, high-priced *maison close*."

I moved forward on my chair. "*Maison close?*" I repeated, wondering what the hell he meant by a closed house.

"*Une maison de plaisirs érotiques*. A fancy brothel. A whorehouse, if you wish, but with class. Expensive carnal luxury for the local elite."

"What?" My eyes must have been the size of two beignets. "Aunt Gabriella?"

He leaned back in his leather chair. His growing smile dug dimples in his clean-shaven cheeks. "She was quite a woman."

I still couldn't believe it. "Gabriella ran a

whorehouse? *That* was her job? ...That has to be illegal, no?"

"Well..." he said, tilting his head repeatedly, "Technically speaking, yes. Brothels are illegal in France. But hers was... and still is... within the confines of the law. Let's just say that my job is to make sure everything's above board. I was Gabriella's private slave when it came to her legal needs," he finished with a glare that made me wonder if he meant it in more ways than one. He rested his elbows on his desk, cupped his manicured hands, and rested his chin on them. "Your aunt was very special, in many ways." A dark cloud passed through his eyes.

I didn't want to think about this hot specimen getting it on with my now deceased aunt (though I wasn't sure if I was misreading him), so I moved the conversation along. "On the phone, you said there was a second person in line to inherit her business. Who would that be?"

He got up. In a few steps, he was standing by the tall windows, looking out toward the street below. His silence tested the limits of my patience.

"Who?" I asked again.

He turned around and his stare met mine. "Me," he finally said.

I cleared my throat and readjusted in my chair. "Isn't it unethical for you to represent my aunt's final wishes when you stand to benefit?"

"*Bien sûr!* Of course!" he exclaimed before lowering his voice. "This entire business is... in the grayest area of the law... But the fewer people in the know, the better. Gabriella arranged it all, and she trusted me to make the best decision at the end of the day. And I hope you can trust me, too."

I tucked a strand of loose hair behind my ear while trying to make sense of it all.

A few seconds passed and I still couldn't. "If you know everything about her business, why didn't she simply give it to you? Why involve me?"

"She knew you'd ask." He returned to his desk. "If you don't mind, I'd like to show you the video she recorded a couple of months ago."

I swallowed hard.

Oh no. A video from beyond? I've barely accepted that she's dead. Am I ready for that?

As though Nicholas could sense my reluctance, he opened his bottom drawer, then pulled out a bottle of whiskey and two tumblers.

"I think we could both use a bit of this," he said, his head nodding toward the golden liquid. "What do you think?"

I let out a sigh while glancing at the expensive Irish bottle. "It's early..." *But then again, seeing my dead aunt on video and later, in just a few hours, watching the love of my life get married?* "Probably wouldn't hurt, considering..."

He smiled at me and poured half an inch in each of the tumblers before handing me one. "To Gabriella, an extraordinary woman who left us too early."

We clinked glasses, then he changed the angle of his monitor so I could see if from my seat. He opened a file on his computer and then enlarged the video player so it occupied the entire screen.

And there she was: Gabriella in a chic baby pink *tailleur*, probably from a well-known designer, as always. Her lit cigarette in her long, slender holder hung from her delicate fingers, its twirling smoke forever frozen in time until Nicholas clicked the play button.

I took a sip. The liquid warmed my dry mouth.

"Dear, if you're watching this," she said before taking a puff and exhaling, "...you and I both know what that means... Which is something more unsettling to me than it is to you now. Well, I hope so anyway... Hell, you have no fucking idea what's been happening with me..."

She took another puff, then extended her arm to set aside her cigarette on what I presumed would be an ashtray just out of the frame. "Anyway, you're probably confused as to why you're in a French lawyer's office, watching a video featuring yours truly."

She paused again, her eyes looking in the direction where she'd left her cigarette.

"Okay, here goes. I realize you and I didn't really know each other. In fact, we were barely more than acquaintances, and I'm sorry about that. I really am... The thing is... I never got close to anybody in our family. Not you. Not your mom. Not even my own parents. But that doesn't matter." She shook her head. "Anyway, last time I saw you, you were different. Somewhere, below that innocent layer you've always impersonated so well, I sensed something... Something that had been awakened... Something we somehow shared. Maybe I was mistaken, but that's unlikely. My instincts are normally right."

She uncrossed her legs, then crossed them opposite (without exposing herself *à la* Sharon Stone in *Basic Instinct*, thankfully.)

"See, I have a somewhat unique business. A certain... personality is required to run it... and to understand its existence in the first place. My intuition has always served me right, in business and in life, and I trust it still can, even though I'm on my last burst of steam."

Gabriella looked away from the camera for a minute, but not toward her cigarette. Her stare was directed up and to the side. When she returned her attention back toward the lens a few seconds later, her eyes glistened with contained tears.

"I've lived a full life. I've got no regrets. But the bulk of it was kept private because society doesn't see my lifestyle and the path I chose as socially appropriate... Maybe things will change in your lifetime? ...I hope so... For your sake."

She brought her right hand to the corner of her right eye, then, with a tissue I hadn't realized she'd been holding, dabbed the tears that were on the verge of running down her face.

"See, I believe that people—men and women— have urges that need to be taken care of. Satisfying carnal needs isn't just a tick in a box, or a dick in a cunt. People are so much more than fleshy orifices. We're curious beings. We all have fantasies. Our urges are much more complex; they run much deeper than our mere physical, raw animal desires. Many people repress them, but some—like me and you—understand that life can be a lot more interesting, pleasurable, and entertaining when we give in to those urges. I see them as a gateway to learning more about ourselves, about what matters in life. I'd even go as far as saying that these urges can help us accept others the way they are... Races, sexual orientations, fetishes, and all the rest..." She chuckled and raised her shoulders. "Maybe my approach would be a great first step toward world peace... But I digress. People who don't repress their urges need a safe place to explore their needs and sexuality. Somewhere where they won't get judged... or where they won't be put in jail for being who they are..."

I brought the glass to my lips. I took a second sip, now that my initial shock had passed.

Aunt Gabriella... Quite a secret keeper that one.

"The thing is," she continued before pausing again with what had to be an impromptu speech. She was rambling way too much for all of this to have been planned. "France is a little ahead of other countries in some ways. Prostitution here has remained legal, but lawmakers have begun a process that I fear is unstoppable. I trust our advantage may soon disappear. So, I expect things will soon get much harder for me and my business...

But I'm certain Nicholas will be clever enough to navigate these hurdles for me... or you, if you're up for it. That legislation may very well happen after I pass." She smiled to an invisible person above the screen, as if trying to get the cameraman's approval to continue.

Was Nicholas there? Was he the one recording?

"But as much as I care and respect him, as a man, as a magic-worker with French laws, and in many, many other ways, I believe I need a woman to run my business. I'm sure Nicholas will help and support you, with whatever you need. He'll teach you the ropes, introduce you to the right people, and lead you so you can become a great business person." A light chuckle escaped her lips. "There's quite a gap between being a flight attendant and a businesswoman... But you've got the goods, the brains, and I'm pretty sure you've also got the curiosity and personality required to do this job well... However, it would involve quite a change. You'd have to move to Paris for one. I'm afraid this isn't a job that can be done remotely, if you know what I mean. But you could transition gradually. I'll let Nicholas fill you in on the details. I hope he can convince you."

She got up, then sat down again.

"There's one more thing... I'd hate myself if I'd forget to mention this... My business, the one I want to hand over to you after I pass, is the best 'job' I've ever had," she said with air quotes. "If you can find a way to make money doing what you like best in the world, you can't ignore that opportunity. For me, this was it. Maybe it can be for you, too. If you decide to knit sweaters for a living, and if it makes you happy, so be it. But I think you may be better fulfilled by doing something along the same lines as what I've done with my life. So please, I urge you to take your time and think it through. Seriously."

She once again turned her attention to that invisible person behind the camera. "Nicholas, please give her plenty of time."

Her gaze then returned to the camera. She leaned forward and pointed her index right at it. "And please... don't ever mention this to your mother." Her eyes were those of an angry parent about to yell at a kid, but then her gaze softened as she once again leaned back on her seat. "She and I have had our differences over the years, probably like most siblings. But from the few attempts I've made at broaching the topic, I know for a fact that she isn't as open-minded as I am, so... Knowing what my real job was could crush her. I'd rather she keeps a fond memory of me, without knowing anything about this part of my life. I hope you understand and can do me this great favor."

After a final pause, she brought her right hand and tapped her heart. "I love you, *sobrinita*. Please pass on my love and best wishes to your mom as well."

3:45 P.M.

THE HOURS FOLLOWING my meeting with Nicholas had been a blur, though a strangely efficient one.

Renée had flocked to the indigo dress in the second shop we'd walked in, saying its cap-sleeves, V-neck, and V-back had been designed for my body shape. A quick change of clothes followed by a twirl in front of the mirror had me agreeing with her. The store attendant recommended a matching pair of shoes and bracelet, both of which they carried in my size. The ensemble was perfect. Never had one of my shopping excursions been so fast and effective. (Nor that expensive.)

So, here we were: two old maids sitting in a cab,

heading to my first and only true love's wedding ceremony, Renée in her burgundy sleeveless dress and me in my new faux-wrap satin gown. She had done up her hair and mine in nonchalant yet formal 'dos. She was the only woman I knew capable of making partially undone chignons look chic. But even knowing that my dress was flattering didn't do a thing to tame my stomach butterflies. Yes, I'd manage to set aside my thoughts about potentially quitting my job and becoming a full-time Parisian businesswoman, which could possibly enable me to afford designer couture like the dress I was wearing on a regular basis. That decision could wait.

But seeing Ady after all those years was no longer avoidable.

Right now, I had to focus on preparing my reaction. I had to muster enough strength and composure to act graciously in front of my ex and his new bride... Or at least stand still without the urge to run away, cry, or scream.

I was taken back to reality when Renée addressed the driver. "*Vous pouvez nous déposer ici, s'il vous plaît.*"

She paid the fare while I exited the cab, carefully holding the satin fabric of my dress so it wouldn't drag on the ground in the process. Once out, I realized we weren't anywhere near a wedding ceremony.

Are we too early and first to arrive? Why did Renée ask the driver to drop us off here? Is the ceremony held in an area where vehicles aren't allowed in? Who knows... And who the fuck cares. I can't believe I'm about to see him after so many years... On his freaking wedding day of all days, ceremonial or not.

Random people walked nearby, chatting in various languages. Some had cameras strapped around their necks, some just appeared to be local people going about their business, taking a stroll in their city. A svelte effeminate man walked with four tiny dogs on pink leashes, followed by a couple holding hands.

Renée squeezed her right arm in the crease of my left elbow.

"Come on," she said.

I lifted the bottom of my dress so it cleared my heels and Renée led me around the majestic Notre-Dame cathedral, whose view helped calm my nerves. At least a little.

A short stroll later, we entered the gardens at the back of cathedral. Thankfully, Renée's cadence had been slow. I hadn't broken a sweat, although each step I'd taken had somehow increased the sense of dread that floated above my head, like a false dark cloud that would mess up this otherwise beautiful day. Sunny days in Paris seemed so rare to me. Most of my visits had been under gray weather or drizzle. Today wasn't hot. It wasn't cold. The temperature was ideal. Above us stretched a solid blue sky, save for a few scattered, puffy white clouds. Seemed luck was on Ady's side. *Hasn't it always been?*

Renée stopped suddenly.

I turned my eyes away from the magnificent cathedral and followed the direction of her gaze.

At first, I saw a mime in a striped white and navy shirt, with white gloves and a black beret crowning his painted-white face. I watched him for a few seconds, but he was immobile. *Crappy mime.* Immobile, save for his eyes, which were locked on something... or someone.

I followed the mime's stare.

And there was Ady, a hundred feet away from Renée and me. A handful of well-dressed people stood around him and his bride. He wore his formal Navy uniform, and the petite woman next to him was dressed in an understated ivory gown. He was still as tall and handsome as I remembered him to be, at least from a distance.

The sight stung my eyes, then my heart.

That could have been me. Why hadn't he loved me as much as I had loved him?

My heart thumped in my chest, its irregular beats fueled by unrecognizable emotions. I concentrated on my breath for a few seconds, trying to keep my eyes dry while doing my best to analyze the mixture of sensations brewing in my gut. Pain, hurt, anger, and disappointment seemed to win over love and lust.

"Want to get closer?" asked Renée.

I swallowed hard, then replied without looking at her, "No."

"Good. Cause the ceremony itself is just for close family."

I turned to face her. "What the fuck? What's wrong with you, Renée? Why are we here then?"

"There's nothing preventing us from witnessing it from a distance! Then, we can follow them to the hotel when they're done."

My hand flew and slapped her shoulder before I could restrain myself.

She smiled at me with the expression of a teenage girl trying to bully her way through life. "I just wanted to see your face while Ady voiced his vows aloud. I don't believe you've forgotten about him like you claim."

"So that's why we're here?" My voice came out louder than I'd hoped. I turned to look at the ceremony and saw a few guests turn our way. I leaned closer to her and whispered, "You want us to crash their ceremony just so you can rub it in my face and prove me wrong?"

She raised her shoulders, but her expression remained cool as steel. "I've run out of ways to entertain myself."

"Quite bitchy of you," I said, staring into her brown eyes. I couldn't recall her ever being that mean to me or anyone in the past.

Her eyes held up my stare, then her eyebrows popped up and she broke eye contact. "Fair enough. Yeah... Probably wasn't cool to force you to come here. Let's head to the hotel and grab a drink instead."

I froze for a second, unsure if I wanted to go through with this. *Why am I doing her this favor? A favor that's inflicting me pain?*

"Come on, my treat. To apologize."

THE NUMBER of people at the reception must have hovered around a hundred.

Among the fashionably dressed guests, I spotted a few acquaintances from way back when. Most appeared to be here with their significant others. Everyone save for Renée, me, and that weird mime from the ceremony. I spotted Luc among the guests, but didn't want to mention it to Renée. He was accompanied by a girl half his age. *Was she the one he cheated on Renée with? Guess it didn't really matter.*

"Why is there a mime here? Is this some sort of French custom?" I asked Renée, hoping to take her attention away from her ex and his guest.

She laughed. "No, silly. What do you think?"

I slowly shook my head at her. "I wouldn't be asking if I knew."

"That's how they met. Looking at the same mime, and then their eyes met. They went for coffee... and the rest is history."

I sighed as my eyes inadvertently rolled.

They even had their meet-cute moment when they fell in love at first sight? Fuck.

What is wrong with the world? ...Or is something wrong with me instead?

My wine glass stared at me, its emptiness unable to solve my inner conundrum.

"I'll go get myself another glass. Want one?" I asked Renée.

"Sure, why not," she replied, not even making eye contact with me. She appeared enthralled by the mime's motions.

As I parted the crowd to make my way back to the bar, I saw a handful of old familiar faces. *Do they remember me?* Then again, it had been so long ago... If they did, they probably wondered why the heck I would have been invited. They probably felt sorry for me or didn't care at all. At least nobody dared to say anything aloud about my presence here.

A few minutes later, I was once again standing next to my only friend in the room, sipping a crisp

Chardonnay, letting its effects smooth out my edgy feelings. Seeing him up close with his new bride when they had entered the room, with guests cheering and clapping loudly, had pinched my heart, but not as much as I thought it would have.

He was still as handsome as I remembered him to be. Sure, maybe his hair had thinned out a bit, but his smile hadn't lost an ounce of charisma. And, I'm slightly ashamed to say, I checked out his ass. Nothing seemed to have changed there. It even brought back a few memories that made me blush.

The bride, Heather, was pretty. Really pretty. Way prettier than Renée had described her to be. And she was quite an intellectual as well. *Good looks and smart. Fuck.* I wish I could have recorded her speech. It was perfect: beautiful, funny, touching... almost sickeningly so.

They say we shouldn't compare ourselves to our exes' new girls, but seriously. Who can resist?

I finished my glass and stared at its bottom before heading back to the bar to get myself another one.

8:23 P.M.

WHILE AT THE BAR, a couple of wine glasses later, a familiar, deep English voice greeted me. "Fancy seeing you here today... After all these years," he said.

I turned around.

It took a second for my drunken eyes to settle on him. Ady was standing less than a foot away from me, champagne flute in hand. So handsome... especially *without* his new petite bride by his side.

"Hi, Ady... Sorry for showing up unannounced. I swear I'm not here to crash your wedding. I'm Renée's last-minute plus one."

"Ah..." was all he said as he nodded.

In a split second, his dark brown eyes dug their

way through my protective layer and pierced my soul, just like they used to.

"Well, I guess congratulations are in order," I said, putting on the biggest smile I could muster and raising my glass, which I realized was empty, yet again. "Toasting with an empty glass is bad luck. Let me rectify that."

I turned to the bartender and ordered another drink. Contradictory feelings fought to the death in the pit of my stomach while I patiently watched the waiter uncork a new bottle for me.

"Still looking good, though. You haven't changed a bit," he said while my attention was focused on the waiter.

I must have reflected on his words for a few seconds too long because by the time I turned around to deliver the smart-ass reply that was on the tip of my tongue, he was gone.

I WAS INEBRIATED enough to withstand the events around me without tipping over, but since I had long lost count of the number of drinks I'd consumed (and I hadn't seen Renée in quite a while), my blacking out point was surely fast approaching.

Did she hook up with someone and leave?

A nagging feeling in the back of my neck made me turn away from the bar. A tall and muscular man was walking toward me. Around forty-five or fifty years old, with long sideburns going all the way to his jaw bone. I'd seen his face before.

What's his name? Kevin?

Whoever he was, he headed my way with

puzzled eyes locked on me as if I was about to save the world with toothpicks or do something significant.

"Here's a bird I hadn't expected to see here. Or ever again, really."

Has to be Cousin Kevin, or another member of Ady's large family I saw once or twice, a long time ago.

"*Votre vin, mademoiselle,*" the waiter said from behind the bar.

I pivoted just enough to grab my drink, then raised my glass at that quasi-stranger who stood in front of me, now with a large smile on his rugged face. "Hear, hear. To miracles and unicorns," I said, smirking at my drunken muse's wit.

He clinked his high-ball glass against mine. "To running into you. Miracle or not."

I downed half of my drink. "I know it's super weird for me to be here... today... at his wedding. Renée roped me into it."

He was shaking his head at me. "Then I'll have to thank her for that."

"Thank her?"

He bridged the small gap between us and squeezed himself sideways next to me along the bar, increasing my level of confusion.

"Why?" I asked as I pressed my hand against his

tuxedo, hoping to push him out of my personal space, but I felt his firm, muscular pecs instead. I reconsidered my instincts. *Hmmm. Cousin Kevin or Whatever-his-name has beefed up.* "Sorry, I'm not sure I remember your name."

"Keith."

"Keith! Of course." *Damn you, girl. You're definitely drunk now.*

He put his drink down on the bar and then his index finger traced my arm. "So, you forgot about me?"

"No, I haven't forgotten about you," I said, taking another sip to try and comprehend what was happening. "I remembered your face. Just forgot your name. Can you blame me, after all these years?"

"Well... I still remember your name," he said as his hand landed on my waist.

I looked down at his arm, then looked back up to meet his gaze. "Really?"

He leaned in and whispered in my ear. "My cousin may have tossed you out, but you've retained a starring role in one of my fantasies," he said, his warm breath caressing my ear and sending quivering waves down my body.

Maybe it was my drunken stupor, but I pulled away and stared him in the eyes. "What?"

He brought me back closer. "I won't repeat myself. Come meet me in the coat check in five, and I'll show you... Or... Miss the opportunity and forever wonder," he said before walking away from the bar.

I watched his large, tall body part the crowd and head out of the room. For a brief second, he turned and made eye contact with me, then he was gone.

What the fuck?

And why the fuck not?

It's not as if I owe anything to Ady. He's freaking married now. Who cares if I fuck his hot cousin?

I scanned the rest of the room. Older relatives I didn't want to talk to. Couples. Couples. And more boring couples. *And... come to think of it, why shouldn't I enjoy my singlehood—being at my ex's wedding or not—and fuck whatever handsome quasi-stranger that presents himself to me?*

Sure, coat check wasn't the most romantic spot, but it could be hot.

Why fucking not?

KEITH WAS LEANING against the wall in the hall just outside the unattended coat check, seemingly waiting for me.

The door had been left wide open. Today having been such a lovely day, it made sense that hardly anyone had brought in—let alone checked— a coat. But a couple of hats had been left on the top shelf.

I walked in and grabbed the nearest one. I put it on and turned around to look at him as he locked us in, leaving the lights on.

"What do you think? Can I pull this look off?"

"Oh... You can leave your hat on, baby," Keith said before closing the gap that separated us.

His lips devoured mine. He smelled and tasted of Old Spice and rum. He forced his body against mine, his hands reaching for my chest, and I stumbled backward. The proximity of the wall prevented me from tumbling on my ass (along with him), but resulted in my head banging against the hard surface. The hat I wore dropped to the floor.

My colliding against the wall had hurt like hell, but I was unsure if I yelped or not. If I did, his hungry lips swallowed any sound that may have left my body. Next thing I knew, my bare breasts hung out of my dress and his erect dick poked through whatever fabric stood between us.

The cocky bastard's fast.

My heart pounded as his thick tongue left my mouth then traced its way down my neck. He moaned while nibbling on my left nipple. I brought my hand up against the back of my head, wondering if I'd cracked it open. I sighed in relief when I saw that my fingers weren't covered in blood. He bit my nipple, then one of his hands reached down toward the bottom of my dress.

"Easy..." I whispered. "Don't bite."

He grunted as he came back to my mouth. He grabbed a hold of my dress and lifted it up around my waist before undoing his pants. "I like it rough—"

"Keith! Keeeiiith! Where are you?" yelled a woman in the hallway. Sounds of high heels rapidly clicking on the marble floor got louder. Her steps were getting closer.

"Fuck," he swore under his breath.

The whiny, nasal-pitched screaming continued. "Keeiiith? Honeeyy, are you here?"

The woman's voice seemed familiar... Then it came back to me. I could picture her face now. I had met her... with Keith... at their house. *That's Keith's wife!*

I pushed him away. "You're married, aren't you?"

He grabbed my ass. "Yeah, so? You knew that. You met me here—"

I slapped him in the face and pushed him again, more forcefully this time. He lost his balance and crashed into the adjacent wall.

"What the fuck? You seemed into it?"

"Sorry, Keith," I said while pulling the fabric of my dress over my breasts and covering myself up again. "Totally forgot you were married. Can't do that. Won't do that. I'm not going to ruin your marriage."

He chuckled. "Who says it's not ruined already? Come on..." he begged, his bare dick pointing at me through the flaps of his shirt, his pants had dropped down to his ankles.

"Not me," I said.

I lowered my dress and ensured my ass wasn't hanging out before storming out of the coat check, leaving him there alone.

Thankfully, his wife seemed to have moved on to another section of the hotel and didn't see me, but I knew my hair had to be a jumbled mess. Seeing a few guests heading my way, I rushed to the ladies' room two doors down from the coat check.

I needed to have a hard stare at myself in the mirror.

A cold-water splash wouldn't hurt either.

GOD, am I glad to have stopped in time!

Well... I guess that depends on one's definition of cheating... But I can't blame myself. I did the right thing. I stopped as soon as I realized.

I inhaled deeply, then exhaled. I repeated the process for a few minutes, my eyes locked on my own reflection.

Who is that woman looking back at me in the mirror?

Who have I become?

Those questions were too deep and too meaningful to be answered now.

Am I already too drunk?

Probably. Nah, most definitely.

I just had to fix my outward self and move on.

At least, my mascara and eye liner had remained intact. My lipstick was long gone, probably transferred onto one of my countless wine glasses. I didn't bring any make up with me to touch it up, so who cared. But my hair was a mess.

After three attempts, I finally remembered how to tie a chignon the way Renée had shown me hours earlier today.

Renée... Where the heck is she?

It's time to find her and go home.

BACK IN THE RECEPTION HALL, after ensuring I was presentable and didn't show any signs of my quasi-extra-marital, coat-check interlude, I ordered myself yet another drink.

Unsure why.

I didn't *need* any more alcohol. Maybe it was just more liquid courage. But it was probably just a habit. It was something to hold on to while I looked for my friend.

I've undoubtably put a fine dent on his open-bar tab. Call it pay back for dumping me by email years ago.

I scoured the room again. Couples, couples, and more couples. *Where did Renée go? Did she leave without telling me?*

I let my eyes settle on the mime doing his 'stuck in a box' routine. It all seemed so ironic to me. 'Marriage and commitment' sure looked like a real box.

...It's a life sentence.

Better hope you pick the right person... or else...

Guess there's always divorce: today's get-out-of-jail-free card.

The mime finally came out of his box and people clapped.

Hmmm, that mime is actually pretty good... Or am I too drunk to notice he sucks?

And come to think of it, he may be cute under that layer of white make-up...

I spotted an empty table closer to him, so I relocated, carefully avoiding familiar faces among the crowd. I paid special attention in avoiding Keith and his wife, but thankfully both were nowhere to be seen.

But not running into them didn't help with the fact that my body had been aroused and left to hang without payoff. I had to release that sexual tension... I scanned the room for men standing alone, away from their lady counterparts and without wedding rings on.

Nobody fit that description.

I returned my attention to the mime.

Maybe he'll do... I can't tell if he's wearing a ring under his white gloves...

Hard to tell what he looks like under all that makeup and those overly expressive faces... but his body certainly shows potential. Tall, not muscular, but not scrawny... He'll do.

So, how do I get his attention?

MY EYES first recognized my open suitcase on the desk in front of the bed where I lay.

Bright light shone through the window, hurting my sleepy eyes, but I couldn't muster the strength to get up and close them.

Fuck! Why didn't I do that when I went to bed last night?

When did I go to bed?

And how the fuck did I get back to my hotel room?

I lifted my head from the pillow but felt a sharp sting on the back of my head. My hand swung to the sore spot. I pressed on it. "Ouch!"

How did I get that fucking bruise?

The coat check incident flashed in my short-term memory. But trying to recall anything else beyond that only served to increase the pinging pain in my cranium.

I rolled over to my side to minimize the light reaching my pupils. But before closing my eyes again, I saw black smudges smeared all over the ivory fabric of the spare pillow next to me.

"What the fuck?"

Sure, I probably forgot to take off my makeup—wouldn't be the first time—but no way my mascara could have stained the pillow case that badly.

In an effort to figure out a logical explanation, I tried to sit up, but at least a minute elapsed before I found my balance. After rubbing my eyes in a last-ditch effort to stop the room from spinning, I spotted my new (and expensive) indigo dress on the carpet. My panties hung on the back of the chair.

"What the fuck?" I repeated, as if the walls could talk and fill me in.

I looked down at my body. *Naked breasts.* I tossed the sheet away from my lower body. *Completely naked... and dirty as hell.*

"Seriously! What the fuck???"

My inner legs were smeared with white and black, and so was the contour sheet under me.

I covered my eyes with my hand, trying to recall the previous night.

Fuck. Black and white make-up. Did I bring the mime home last night?

I could not recall a damn thing.

Maybe this is just a nightmare and it will all make sense when I wake up in a few hours.

SOMEWHERE IN THE DISTANCE, my phone rang. The familiar ringtone blasted through my ear drums as though a nuclear alarm had gone off.

"Shut up!" I yelled at the device, knowing fair well that it wouldn't do anything to stop it, but it somehow made me feel a little better.

Maybe Siri has a command for that?

I flapped the sheet away from my body, exposing my white-painted thighs and confirming my earlier memories were real, then walked over to the damned device.

"Hello?" I said after finally quieting it down.

"*Bonjour, c'est Nicholas.* Are you ready to go visit

your aunt's business? I could pick you up in about fifteen minutes?"

"Oh... Fuck... Sorry... *Désolée...* I totally forgot about it. Hmm... Any way to reschedule for a little later today?"

"Ah! Did you have a nice evening out on the town last night? I understand. Why don't you call me when you feel rested and ready to go?"

"Will do."

"*Au revoir... et bonne nuit, ma chère! Faites de beaux rêves.*" I heard him say just as I pressed the button to hang up.

Yeah, yeah...

I turned off my ringer and all notifications.

Doubt my dreams will be sweet, but I'll definitely try to get some sleep.

Maybe some of last night's blacked-out events will have reinserted themselves in my memory by the time I get up again.

I closed the curtains in one fell swoop, then crashed back on my bed, this time in total obscurity.

5:00 P.M.

"I WAS BEGINNING to think you'd forgotten about me," he said in a tone that had me wondering if I'd totally messed up and if he'd be sending me an invoice for a full day's worth of work.

"I'm so sorry," I repeated. "I swear this is not typical behavior on my part. It's just..." Weighing the pros and cons of divulging the truth was too difficult for my hung-over mind. *Fuck it. Truth is nearly always better.* "Last night, the long-lost love of my life got married. I over-indulged, if you know what I mean..."

"Ah? Well, glad you're finally awake then. One would assume this situation will only present itself once. So... You're forgiven. Don't worry about it."

A wave of relief came over me. "Thank you for understanding."

"That being said, we've got a slight problem with our new timeline. We can still tour your aunt's business, but by the time we'll get there, some patrons will have arrived, so we'll both need to blend in as to not break the illusion of—"

"What?"

"You'll understand when we get there. Would it be fair for me to assume that *Mademoiselle* Gabriella's body size and shape is similar to yours? I could pick up one of her outfits for you to wear?"

I had to think about it for a second. "We're probably about the same size, but I'm a few inches taller, if that matters."

"Perfect. I'll swing by your hotel in about fifty minutes."

After hanging up with Nicholas, I checked my messages. Renée had left me five of them, all of which were long-winded and apologetic.

The gist? She'd left early without telling me because she'd hooked up with Luc. Again. She was sorry for having dragged me back into Ady's life. Not cool of her. She should have given me a heads-up before she left... *Blah, blah, blah.*

Well, she'd have to wait for me to get over my

hangover (and to get over how bitchy she acted) before she'd get a phone call back from me. She didn't need to know the sad end to my evening... And she'd be unable to fill me in on the details I still couldn't—and probably never would—recall.

After taking something for what was left of my hangover headache, I showered and tidied my room the best I could to hide the evidence of my shameful behavior.

Then, I changed into my jeans and T-shirt and dried my hair.

I was grateful Nicholas had offered to bring me an outfit—whatever it was going to be—but I was curious to learn why I needed to wear something special.

FIRST THE RECEPTION called to confirm I was expecting a guest, then he was at my door two minutes later, dressed in a full tuxedo, one of those opaque suit protector cases in one hand and a square box in the other.

"Wow! You sure clean up nice!" I said. "Come in."

"Here's something your aunt loved wearing, along with a coat," he said, handing me the thick but light case.

"A coat? Is it cold out today?" I asked.

He shook his head, and I took a few steps toward the bed to lay the case flat on the comforter before unzipping the cover. Two hangers. The first held a very long charcoal-gray trench coat. I pulled it out of the case, exposing the second item: a semi-sheer black outfit that would likely be sold in the lingerie section of a very expensive boutique. I pulled it out and held it up against the light.

Well, at least there were some *opaque parts to it.*

"I see..."

"You're fine with wearing it?" he asked. "Cause if you're not, then there's no pressure. And there's probably no point in visiting your aunt's business if the outfit alone makes you uncomfortable."

"I'll go and put it on," I said with a smile before heading to the bathroom.

A few minutes later, after realizing the outfit didn't leave room for any underwear to be worn with it, I came out and twirled in front of my lawyer in his penguin suit.

"You actually pull this off. I'm impressed," he said, quietly clapping his hands. "Now, *la pièce de résistance*..." He opened the box he'd dropped on the corner of my desk and walked toward me.

The white fabric box contained two golden masks with jewels embedded in them. I lifted the first one. Heavier than I had expected.

"They're not real stones, are they?" I asked

while bringing it to my face and wrapping the three sturdy elastic bands around the back of my head.

"Real precious stones and three types of gold, but it's only dipped in gold. Otherwise it would be too heavy to wear."

"Really? How much is it worth?"

"Much less than your aunt's business," he said before taking out a second mask from the box, this one more masculine. In doing so, he exposed another object previously hidden underneath it. "And this is for you as well."

Resting on the black velvet was a gorgeous golden necklace with stones matching those of the mask I was wearing.

"Let me," he said after placing his own mask on the comforter and extracting the necklace from the box.

He dropped the box on the bed, then lifted my hair away from my neck and placed it on my right shoulder, then dropped the heavy necklace around my neck and clasped it behind my back. "Now, go and have a look at yourself with the complete outfit on," he said, pointing me toward the full-length mirror on the back of my bathroom door.

I walked the short distance to the mirror, the long slit that went up to my hip along one side of the dress allowed for long, unrestricted strides. I was stunned by the woman I saw in front of me. The baroque mask only covered my eyes and nose. My mouth was unobstructed. And this necklace...

"*Magnifique. Mademoiselle Gabriella serait ravie de vous voir ainsi,*" he said.

I turned to face him just in time to see a familiar black cloud return to his eyes.

"Nicholas, I've been meaning to ask you..."

He looked at me "What?"

"A few things really... But how did she die?"

"She was really sick—"

"But I didn't know anything. My mother never told me she was sick."

"I don't believe she told anyone. Gabriella was a very private person."

I let that sink in for a few seconds. Maybe that's where I got that trait from. "Sick with what?"

"Lung cancer that remained undiagnosed for too long. It spread to other organs. Her odds were meek."

"But didn't she want to do chemo? Or wasn't there a treatment she could have done to stop it?"

He shook his head. "It was too little too late for her. She wanted to live life to the fullest until the end."

"So, when I last saw her, she knew she was dying..."

He nodded, then looked away, but not before I noticed the tears forming in his eyes. I wanted to ask him if there'd been something between him and her. There had to have been something. Something quite special really...

"Let's get going," he said before removing the trench coat from the hanger and holding it up for me to slip into.

NICHOLAS DROVE A LUXURIOUS BMW. Gray and practical as opposed to something red and loud he could have probably purchased for the same price. *Or maybe he owns one of those as well?*

He gave me a little bit of history about Gabriella's business on our way there, but I couldn't seem to focus on any of what he was saying; my mind was still vainly trying to piece together my previous evening.

I don't even know—or recall—that mime's name!

On my lap, the weight of the box that contained our masks brought me back to the moment.

"Should I be worried about someone stealing

my mask?" I asked him as he turned off from a main street and headed down a tree-lined, narrow, cobbled-stoned road.

"No. Our patrons are wealthy. We run thorough security checks on them. Criminal records, financial statements, medical screening, the whole lot."

"Isn't it illegal to request all of that information?"

"And aren't brothels illegal?" he asked rhetorically. "Our employees are run through the same checks, and they are paid very well, especially for their silence. Our patrons appreciate the peace of mind and confidentiality of our business. They pay very good money to be members of our establishment, and if our rules don't work for them, they're not allowed in."

"And how much money are we talking about? How much does the business make?"

He grinned and kept quiet.

As he turned into a small driveway, a black metal gate appeared before us. He stopped the car, rolled down his window, and pressed a button before saying his name aloud.

The gate's mechanism clicked loudly, then the doors opened slowly in front of us. He rolled in, and I watched the gates close behind us through the passenger's mirror while Nicholas kept going forward. The moment they were closed, I returned my attention to the road in front of us. What I saw made me gasp.

"The business could probably afford one of these buildings every year," he said as I almost drooled watching more and more of the beautiful architecture appear in front of my eyes. It was three stories high, built in a style reminiscent of the *Château de Versailles*. My eyes continued their inspection of the property until they reached a wall.

The gardens aren't as extensive though, but who cares! I doubt people come here to take a stroll in the garden. Or do they?

"Holy shit!" I couldn't help myself.

"Yes. Serious money. I can show you financial figures later if you want. But first, I'll give you a tour of the property. Please put on your mask and hand me mine when I stop the car," he said as he drove around to the front of the property. Once our wheels stopped, a valet instantly walked to the car and opened my door to let me out. Then, after holding my hand as I stepped out in my high heels, he closed my door and guided me up the steps before going back to the car and taking a seat in the driver's side.

By then, Nicholas had already joined me by the front door.

As if someone had been monitoring our entrance, the heavy wooden door opened for us and a man's voice welcomed us: "*Bonsoir Monsieur Nicholas.*" He turned to me, then added, "*Mademoiselle.*"

"*Bonsoir,*" Nicholas said with a head nod.

I followed suit and greeted the man. Nicholas then turned to me, and I understood it was time to take off my trench coat. One arm at a time, he helped me peel away my only opaque layer, then he handed my coat to the man who had opened the door for us.

"Let's begin our grand tour!" he said.

I followed him down the marble entrance hall; our footsteps echoed against the tall, intricately carved wooden walls.

A few moments later, we began our ascent on the wide marble stairs. I kept a hand on the balustrade to avoid falling off while looking around me. Then, I saw her: dead center in front of us on the first landing, a large oil painting of what seemed to be Gabriella surrounded by a handful of women, all wearing beautiful masks, scant clothing, and stilettos.

6:50 P.M.

THE FIRST ROOM we stopped in, which Nicholas called *le salon*, reminded me of the British tea room I'd seen in that very special Irish castle a while back. Except that it was probably three times as spacious.

According to my lawyer-turned-official-tour-guide, this room was meant as a mingling room for guests to interact with the staff shortly after they arrived. But right now, it was empty, save for Nicholas, me, and a couple of men in white shirts with simple black masks standing behind an ornate wooden bar that occupied half of the back wall. I recognized several premium brands among the large selection of bottles held on the shelves behind them. The rest of the room was expansive enough for about twenty or thirty people to sit comfortably in various, fairly isolated areas. There were couches, love seats, and even mattresses surrounded by sheer curtains. A few sizable plants, vases, and other decorative elements offered some added privacy, at least from certain angles.

"Let's try and show you more of the property before the first guests arrive," Nicholas said before wrapping his arm around my waist and leading me out of the room, greeting the bartenders on the way.

He pushed a swinging door and we ended up in a narrow hall, which winded a few times then went up two steps before opening into a wider passageway. A dozen doors lined each side.

"And here are some of the bedrooms for our guests to use as they see fit," he said. "There's also another level, which can be reached if you go all the way to the end of the hallway. There's another wide staircase there."

But it seemed we weren't going to go there. Nicholas had stopped in front of the first door on our left then opened it. He walked in, and I followed him.

I imagined that's how one of the rooms at the Ritz would look like, having never stayed at one of their hotels. Luxury oozed from every detail. Thick, velvety embroidered fabric hung in decadent loops over the tall windows, which sheer curtains currently covered. Another layer of thick burgundy fabric was nested on the outer edges, ready to enclose the room into obscurity should the guests want it. A Victorian-era settee, two padded chairs, a long coffee table, and a large fireplace occupied half the room while the other half was presided over by a king-size bed whose ornate and massive foot had seemingly been painted with gold. At the head of the bed, a luxuriously padded oval reigned, crowned with a thickset gold seal. The same fabric that had been used to upholster the headboard hung in loose hoops several feet above the bed, its edges decorated with golden trim and ending with two large tassels, one on each side. A dozen decorative pillows of assorted shapes and sizes had been piled on the bed. But the details that I liked most were the intricate moldings on the wall. A light baby blue covered the larger, plainer areas, but the trims had been painted white and some of the detailed carvings, in gold.

"Are all the rooms just like this one?"

He looked around before replying. "More or less. We can visit a few more later if you'd like. But first, let me show you something." He headed back toward the open door so I followed, but I was taken by surprise when he closed then locked the door instead.

"Sorry!" I said as I walked into him. "What are you doing? Didn't you say you wanted to show me something?"

He turned around and faced me. "In here, but I don't want anyone else to know," he said before proceeding to the wall next to the fireplace. He pulled a small table away from the wall, then pressed one of the wooden carvings in the dado railing about a third of the way up the wall. A section of the wall panel receded. He pushed it in further.

"Won't people get suspicious when they see the door is locked?"

"What do you think? They'll assume we got *busy*." He smiled. "Come and follow me," he said before sliding into the small space.

At first I hesitated. Confined spaces didn't scare me per se, but this gap didn't appear to be any deeper than a foot, and it seemed pitch-black in there... But this secret passageway had aroused my curiosity.

First having to wear masks, then this...

Gabriella sure had lots of secrets in her life.

I stepped in on the plush carpeted floor, and then Nicholas's arm brushed against my chest as he moved the entrance panel to close it again.

All of a sudden, a series of very small lights brightened up the edges of the floor, just like the emergency aisle-lighting system I was familiar with on planes.

"Follow me," he repeated.

And I did.

I WAS sure glad *not* to suffer from claustrophobia.

What felt like fifteen-minutes later, after he had pointed to several hidden panels and sliding openings along the narrow passageway, Nicholas stopped.

The lights along the edges of the floor indicated we'd reached a dead-end. But a soft beeping sound made me look up. My tour guide was punching numbers in a backlit keypad on the wall.

Shortly after pressing the last digit, a latch came undone, its click partly muffled by the plush carpet.

Nicholas pushed the wall in front of us.

Another hidden door.

Light once again reached my pupils, making me squint while my eyesight adjusted. It wasn't daylight. More like that blue light that TV sets emitted in a dark room at night. But I nonetheless felt a wave of relief as I left the confined hallway and followed Nicholas into the larger space.

More than a dozen monitors had been tiled on one of the walls. *Is this a control room?*

I turned around and realized it couldn't be—or at least it couldn't be *just* that.

There was an entire bedroom in here, with a king-sized bed covered by a dozen pillows, a tall wardrobe, a dresser, a few closed doors leading to who knows where. Heavy curtains that went from floor to ceiling covered the wall next to the control monitors.

Nicholas walked toward the bed while taking off his mask, which he then dropped on top of the ivory comforter. "This was Gabriella's bedroom." He continued his trajectory and crossed the room to reach the curtains. With a light screeching sound, he pushed a set open, and a stream of what remained of the sun's rays poured in. He unlocked the clasp on the large windows and pushed them open, then looked at me. "Come and have a look."

I obeyed and dropped my mask on the bed as

well. A light breeze caressed my face and brushed the light fabric of my outfit against my body. The view was stunning. A couple of acres of beautifully tended gardens expanded in front of the balcony onto which Nicholas and I stood. Sure, in the distance the city continued its sprawl, but I felt like we were in a private oasis, just out of the city.

The size of the land alone has to be worth a fortune... Then the luxurious building on top of it. No wonder Gabriella was always dressed in the latest trends!

"Beautiful, no?" Nicholas asked.

I let out a long sigh. "Incredible is more like it. Did she live here full-time?"

"No. But she spent most weekends here. And some weeknights when special events were hosted."

"Where did she live the rest of the time?"

His eyebrows lifted and his Adam's apple jerked as he swallowed. "You know... Here, there... Other people's apartments..." His gaze then settled on the garden in front of us.

"You mean she regularly hooked up with... clients?"

He nodded slowly, his silence seemingly burdened by a secret that had become too heavy to bear.

"Were you one of her lovers?" I asked.

He turned to face me, tears in his eyes. "Yes. I loved her very much."

I wrapped my arm around his waist and rested my head against his chest, carefully avoiding my sore spot. "I'm sorry you lost her so soon," I said to him.

He reciprocated, wrapping his arm around my shoulders.

A few minutes elapsed while we stayed in a comforting embrace on the balcony.

Guess he's like my uncle or something...

We watched the last stream of light disappear and he tapped me on the shoulders before dropping his arm away from my body.

"Anyway. Let's finish the tour so you get a sense of what happens here."

He walked back in the room, and I followed him.

He closed the curtains then locked the doors behind me.

"Security monitors don't cover every part of the property, but as you saw through the multiple sliding panels in the secret passageway we came in from, Gabriella could peek on pretty much every room in this place. The employees don't know how to reach this room, and it needs to stay this way. Our guests sign a release form. They're aware nothing is private here; they know video cameras or similar equipment are used to monitor the premises, but they know none of it will ever be released, unless we're legally obligated to. That's why I asked you to wear a mask. Since you haven't officially accepted the... job... if you want to call it that... Or ownership of the business? ...Anyway, I didn't want you to be connected to it in the event someone decides to shut us down and come after those who knew of the business's existence."

"So how many employees are we talking about, and what kind?"

He walked toward the monitors. "A few cooks, bartenders, and gardeners, but most of our staff consists of our very special women," he said while pointing at a specific screen which displayed about twenty women in outfits similar to the one I wore. They were pampering themselves up, applying makeup and straightening their hair in what appeared to be a large change room complete with those mirrors outlined with large light bulbs I imagined famous actors used in their dressing rooms.

I moved my eyes to the next screen. On it, a handful of women had already taken seats in the *salon*, their colorful masks also secured by strings around the backs of their heads. The women weren't positioned near each other, though. Instead, they were peppered throughout the room, a cocktail in hand, as if socializing among themselves wasn't permitted. A man dressed in a tuxedo appeared into the frame and joined one of the ladies. He too wore a mask, not just hiding his eyes, but obscuring his entire face.

"A customer," Nicholas said, noticing what I was looking at.

Over the next few minutes, more and more men appeared in the *salon*, where most employees had moved to. Only a handful of women were left in the change room, based on the security footage we were watching.

"That's all live?" I asked.

"Of course."

"What kind of people come here? I mean are they locals?"

"Most live in Paris, at least part-time. We have several high executives in the fashion industry, politicians, entrepreneurs, self-made millionaires..."

I scanned the rest of the monitors so I'd get a

better understanding of his business proposition. "So where are the male employees?"

He laughed at my question, then cocked his head at me when I repeated myself.

"Men are our target market. Straight men," he said.

My arms flung up. "So? You mean you've never thought of including women customers and men employees? And what about homosexual guests?"

"We've had special evenings with a few hand-selected men... But those were rare occurrences."

A groan escaped my lips before I could restrain myself. "What about women patrons?"

One of his eyebrows went up, then he frowned and shook his head. "Not many women openly cheat on their husbands like that. At least not here."

"What do you mean? All of these men..." I said, pointing at the monitor showing them flirting with the female employees. "*All* of them are married?"

"Well, no. But many of them are."

"What?" I brought my hand to my forehead but kept staring at the monitors in front of me.

Why does everything have to do with marriage and cheating bastards these days?

Is it just me who's so behind and old-fashioned about this? Have marriage vows become meaningless to everyone?

I'm not opposed to people exploring their sexuality and trying out new things, new people... But it must be done in all honesty, especially if it involves consequences with a mate, someone you've made a promise to.

Sure, I'm not sharing any of that information with my family. I totally understand and agree with Gabriella's request about keeping this from my mom. And my lifestyle is definitely not something I'd like to share with my dad either. His little girl would be forever tainted in his mind.

If I were married, though... I'd like to think I'd have married an open-minded person who'd accompany me in this adventure.

Yeah, an open-marriage of sorts... Could such a marriage work?

"Should we continue the tour?" Nicholas asked, taking me out of my head.

I sighed. "I guess so. Where do these other doors lead to?" I asked while pointing to the opposite wall.

"The passageway we came through only grants us access to some of the rooms. There are other passageways that lead to the other side of the hallway, and another that grants us access to the rooms upstairs, but they both involve climbing up and down ladders, so I thought it'd be better for us to come through the one we used. If you decide to take over the business, you'd be welcome to explore all of them as you wish, whenever you want."

He walked to one of the doors and opened it. "But this one is the bathroom, should you need to use it."

I shook my head.

"Well, what do you say we go and mingle. Experience the business for yourself?" he asked. "But no obligation. You could interact with a few guests so you understand if they're happy with the services here?"

"You mean run a customer satisfaction survey?" I asked.

He grabbed both of our masks from the bed then handed me mine. "As long as you promise not to give out questionnaires. That would kill the mood."

"And you say you don't have a sense of humor," I said, jabbing two fingers in his stomach. Its firmness took me by surprise. *Hmmm. Gabriella probably had some good times with him.* I followed him back out of the room, and the door locked automatically behind me.

Somehow, the passageway didn't seem so intimidating on the way back. The walls were not paper-thin, but they were certainly not insulated enough to hide the rooms' occupancy status. I stopped in my tracks when I heard a woman's longing moans on my right. I felt the wall, hoping to find one of those sliding panels Nicholas had pointed to earlier.

A few seconds later, I did.

I slid it open and lined my eyes behind the two peepholes.

At first, I only saw an empty bed and thought I hadn't found the right room, but then a hand flew up about two feet from my observation point in the wall. I readjusted—or at least I tried. The guests seemed either too low or too close to the wall for me to see anything. Then something—more likely someone—rammed into the wall, making the whole passageway shake. The grunts that ensued clarified that I'd see nothing from that peephole since that couple was obviously fucking against my wall.

Nicholas tapped me on the shoulder then, through the faint light, I saw his fingers motion to follow him.

A moment later, we were back in the original bedroom we'd walked in before I'd found out about my aunt's voyeurism fetish.

"So, again. Please keep that secret room and

passageway to yourself. Guests and employees are in no way to be privileged to that information."

"Of course!"

"Now, what do you want to do? We can mingle and have fun, or I can show you the books and employee roster... Or we can put an end to this tour if you're not interested."

He continued his path toward the door, and I thought about my options while following him.

I couldn't say I wasn't interested *at all*, but the thing that bothered me most wouldn't be resolved by looking at some books. Unless my aunt was also involved in some illegal drug trafficking, it was clear from the property alone that she made a lot of money. I needed to talk to the guests and find out if they were all married men looking for a way to cheat on their wives without getting caught, or if there was more to it. Or maybe I wanted to find reassurance that my new way of living had a potential future with a man... *Whatever.* If I found a handsome single man back in the *salon*, then what harm would there be in spending a few minutes toward the pursuit of some mutual, heavenly carnal fun?

After all, I was all dressed up for the part.

Having nowhere to go—or come—was certainly not the most wanted outcome here.

"First option would be better," I said a few steps after we'd returned to the main passageway.

"To the *salon*, then," he said before elegantly pointing me back the way we'd come from.

BACK IN THE *SALON*, I scoped out my options.

It was obviously a one-way menu where women sat pretty and waited until a man approached them. I decided to challenge that approach. Instead of looking for an empty seat, I glanced around and looked for unmarried men. (Not that rings couldn't be removed, but at least I narrowed down my choices to a handful of men without rings—or tan lines—on their fourth fingers.)

I settled on a blond, pony-tailed man with a charming smile. It was hard to gage a man's age when he had a mask on, but as I walked toward him, I saw no obvious crow's feet around his bright emerald-green eyes. He was probably 25 or 30 years old.

"*Bonsoir,*" he said, smiling back at me.

It suddenly dawned on me I had to pretend to be French. "*Bonsoir,*" I said with my best accent.

"*Vous êtes nouvelle, non?*" he asked, wondering if I was a new girl.

"*Oui. Vous êtes un régulier?*" I tried to keep my smile on while mentally rolling my eyes at my bad conversation skills. *Of course, he's a regular client... It's not like I was standing in a neighborhood bar where anyone and everyone could walk in.*

"*Lorsqu'une chose nous plaît, il faut revenir,*" he said, referring to how much he liked the place, so that's why he kept coming back. "*Alors pourquoi n'aprennons-nous pas à mieux nous connaître?*" he asked, pointing to the door leading out of the room, toward the main hallway I'd accessed earlier with Nicholas.

His invitation to get to know each other certainly was a polite way to present his intentions... But once again, no surprise considering where we were standing... and how I was dressed.

I looked down at my sheer outfit once more.

Aunt Gabriella's outfit.

This whole thing's surreal.

He placed his hand on the small of my back

and led me out of the room. Just as we passed the bar, he asked, "*Vous voulez un verre de champagne?*"

"*Pourquoi pas?*" I replied, not seeing a reason to turn down a drink right now. After all, they say it's the best cure to a hangover, and I had to try the full experience.

"*Attendez-moi ici. Je reviens tout de suite.*"

I waited where I stood. Just as he'd promised, he came back ten seconds later with two flutes of champagne. He hadn't paid or tipped the tall bartender.

Guess this is an 'all-inclusive' private club... With lightning-fast service!

I wonder if those bartenders offer services in addition to drinks? Or maybe they entertain themselves with some of the hostesses during slow times?

My Frenchman handed me my drink and we clinked glasses. "Santé!" we said simultaneously.

I took a sip, and he grabbed me by the waist. "*Allons boire notre verre sur un balcon. Ça vous plairait?*"

I smiled and nodded, agreeing to his offer to go and drink on a balcony somewhere.

We left the room and headed toward the familiar main hallway where the rooms were located. On our way there, we crossed another couple. They were clearly done for now: him with his bowtie untied around his neck, his shirt not fully done; her with her rosy cheeks and ruffled hair. Polite nods were exchanged in silence.

We walked past the bedroom I had visited earlier with Nicholas, and I followed my guy through another door that had been left ajar. The room was empty, and the bed was still made.

Are there maids who take care of changing linen throughout the night?

Or are people assigned their own room?

So many questions to ask Nicholas, but I forced myself to return to the present moment, to be mindful.

My emerald-eyed man placed his drink on a small table, then took off his tuxedo jacket and hung it on the back of a chair. He then walked over to the curtains and opened them up. His ass certainly appeared round and firm, his shoulders broad.

I couldn't wait to have a feel.

He opened the tall doors, grabbed his drink again, finished it, and then put the empty glass down. He stepped onto the balcony. "*Venez. La vue est magnifique,*" he said, ordering me to join him and enjoy the beautiful scenery.

I walked toward him after taking another sip and getting rid of my empty glass.

This room's balcony was smaller than the one in my aunt's bedroom, and it faced a different side of the property, but he was right. The view was stunning, both when I looked out of the balcony and after, when I turned around and faced my mysterious masked man. We were so close; I could feel the warmth of his mint-scented breath on my cheeks.

Who is he? A fashion designer? A banker? ...But does it matter and do I really want to know?

With a lone finger, he slipped one of my straps down my shoulder and traced my shoulder bone a few times before diving down into my cleavage. He moved in closer, pushing his tall and firm body against mine. My lower back rested against the top of the guardrail. His excitement transcended the layers of clothing that separated us.

I undid his belt, then his zipper before scooping a hand down his soft underwear. A firm, thick dick twitched in my hand as my fingers wrapped themselves around his girth.

He let out a deep breath, blowing warm air onto my neck. While one of his hands was still exploring my breasts, his other hand flicked my hair behind my neck and he bent down to kiss my ear. He nibbled on my earlobe, and I let my head go backward a little, enough for me to see the large moon above us. Its light brightened up the sky for a few seconds before it got partly covered by clouds.

He spun me around to face the guardrail and lifted the back of my dress.

"*Ah, mais quel cul!*" he said before slapping my ass.

I felt my cheeks warm up from the compliment. "*Merci,*" I said, shaking my praised booty a little.

I readjusted my mask and rested my hands on the guardrail while he massaged my ass and then parted my cheeks. He let out a groan then let go of me. A ripping sound followed. *Unwrapping a condom?*

A few seconds later, I felt the tip of his cock slide back and forth below my pussy. I raised my ass and arched my back to grant him a better angle, which he accepted in one slow and highly lubricated swoop. *The vibe in this place leaves very little need for foreplay, well at least when it comes to me and my hormones.*

A yelp escaped my lips as his long shaft bumped against the back of my insides, but it didn't stop him. Instead, he pulled out and reinserted himself a little faster, but thankfully not as deeply this time.

I delighted in our bodies meshing so perfectly,

my breathing loud and slow at first. Then he added a few sharp slaps on my ass, each time taking me by surprise, forcing my insides to inadvertently clench against his shaft. And each time, it took me a little closer to my finish line.

He was the silent type, save for his breathing and the clapping sounds he made on my ass. But his cadence was also speeding up and his thrusts were getting deeper. Except for the odd slaps, he had mostly kept his hands on my hips. When he let go of me again, I half expected to get slapped, and even clenched my insides, but instead his warm breath brushed my back, and then I felt his hands on my breasts. He pressed them, forcing me to unfold my upper body and stand up more. I did, at least as much as I could while keeping him inside of me.

A loud male groan made me turn my head to the right.

Two balconies down, others were enjoying the peaceful night sky. At first I only saw a woman standing next to a man, kissing him. *But this doesn't make sense. How can he groan so loudly while his mouth's busy?* Then I looked down and saw another woman, this one bent in half at the hip. She held on to the kissing man's hip as her head bobbed forward and back in front of his crotch. Then, I looked behind that woman. Standing on the balcony, in the doorway to the room was another man, fucking that woman in the ass.

Guess this maison close *is a little more flexible than I thought. It's not limited to one-on-one action...*

But my emerald-eyed man had noticed my distraction. He slapped me on the ass again, then pulled away from me before spinning me around to face him. He grunted at me, his eyes now displaying a fiercer, predatory quality.

A wave of disappointment surged through me. My pussy wanted his cock back as much as I needed air to breathe.

"I need you to fuck me hard!" I ordered.

"*Quoi?*" he asked, reminding me I was in France.

I shook my head, trying to recall my French sex talk, but the only thing that came was "*Prends-moi.*"

His strong hands got a hold of my ass and he lifted me up. I wrapped my legs around his hips.

Another spin and a few steps later, he had me pinned against the outside wall. His dick finished me off within a few delicious, powerful thrusts. He came a few seconds later, loudly exhaling into my ear while I was still quivering from my own bliss, looking out toward Paris's beautiful skyline.

9:30 P.M.

THE CAR RIDE back was spent in silence.

Nicholas had fulfilled the promise he'd made to Gabriella. He'd shown me her business, books, finances, etc. He'd answered all my questions. It all seemed very appealing... Very appealing indeed, if it weren't for one important flaw: it catered almost exclusively to married men who wanted to cheat on their wives.

And right now, that one flaw went against my core beliefs.

"So, what do you think?" he asked as he double-parked his car in front of my hotel, its blinkers gently ticking away the seconds I needed to make up my mind for good.

I undid my seatbelt and turned to face him.

"Very enticing..." I opened my door and stepped out before putting down the box containing both of our masks on the passenger seat. "But I think I'll have to pass."

His eyes remained still, but he swallowed hard.

"Very well then. Keep the dress, necklace, and coat. Have a good night and a safe flight back tomorrow."

"Thank you, Nicholas. Have a good night, too," I said before closing the door.

And just like that, he was gone, his tail lights quickly disappearing.

A cloud of dread and guilt began to occupy the void his offer—Gabriella's final wishes—had created.

10:25 A.M.

PHONE IN HAND, I couldn't bring myself to remove my French SIM card and replace it with my regular Virgin Mobile one. All I could do was stare at my screen.

For a brief instant, I made eye contact with the man sitting across from me at the departure gate. Beautiful green eyes. But it couldn't be my guy from the night before. His hair was short and brown.

We broke eye contact when he turned to kiss the woman sitting next to him. I looked down at his fingers.

Wedding ring.

Marriage can't help but fuck with one's mind. Watching happy people tie the knot surrounded by their closest friends and family was hardly a sore predicament, but getting married was just one day. One happy party-like event (with or without religious baggage). But when those first-day celebrations ended, a long life together began where nothing else in the world had changed. Getting married only meant getting on the ramp to a long and repetitive life where routine and boredom undoubtedly ended up murdering whatever passion and lust may have existed in the first place.

...Is this what leads married people to cheat?

Then again, people who aren't married also cheat on their partners...

My current way of living, of experiencing men (and sometimes women), was probably more exciting in the long run. Probably easier to find carnal happiness than find "true love" (if that even existed). *Fulfilling? Physically: yes, most times. Emotionally: it certainly has its fair share of highs and lows.*

But everything does.

The perfect relationship—marriage, boyfriend, one-night stand, regular sex buddy—didn't exist. After questioning myself over the past few months, I'd settled on the following perfect arrangement:

Finding a hot guy who was open-minded enough to let me explore my sexual horizons, possibly accompanying me along the way, but not exclusively. But that person could also be there for me at times, to fill needs other than my sexual ones. We could discuss things, intelligently. I didn't know if that man even existed and knew even less about how to find him. Putting this up on an online profile would certainly attract a herd of creeps, from horny teenagers wanting a cougar, to never-leave-their-mom's-basement porn addicts... And describing my needs as anything else would be misleading men and attracting those vanilla-types who want to start a family and get on the regular program that now seemed so boring to me.

It was unthinkable for me to settle for that now.

I should really thank Alex for broadening my horizons on that Toronto flight way back when. Thinking back about the past few months warmed my cheeks.

Will I ever stop blushing for no reason?

Who cares? I've certainly come a long way.

The tall French stewardess boarding my upcoming flight began her pre-departure announcement, inviting families traveling with children to line up. I didn't know her. I couldn't tell if she led an exciting life, but I was certainly fond of the work we shared. It was quite a job really. *Lots of perks. Could I give it up?*

Would living in Paris be as exciting?

Maybe...

Would running an already successful business and making loads of money be appealing?

Certainly.

But supporting a business where only rich men could cheat on their wives seemed wrong...

But what if the odds were evened out. What if the business could be turned into something I'd be able to support with my heart and soul? Something where everyone stands to win...

I unlocked my screen, then looked at my list of recent calls before dialing Nicholas's number. The call rang without answer, but I left a voicemail:

"Nicholas, c'est moi. S'il vous plaît, oubliez ce que je vous ai dit hier soir. J'ai besoin d'un peu plus de temps pour y penser. Je vous rappelle dès que j'aurai pris ma décision finale, d'accord? À très bientôt j'espère."

PART TWO

MY XXX EXPERIENCE

THE PLAN

AFTER CAREFULLY COPYING HER WORDS—WEIRD accents and all—into Google Translate, I discovered that she asked Nicolas to give her more time to think it through.

My stewardess could one day leave her job to become a whorehouse manager—or whatever they call those people—but I've already read her remaining three journal entries. She traveled to other countries after Paris, so I'm obviously getting outdated news through her journal.

That being said, I believe my luck is about to change. She left me too many leads, too many details. One of them has to bear fruit this time. Here are my options:

. . .

OPTION 1: Track down Gabriella Andrews's obituary.

Determining the date of her death will give me a timeline of sorts. I should be able to figure out at least the month and year her Paris journal entry was written. As for getting my stewardess's name, the woman's related to her on her mother's side, so that probably means shit for last names. Unless she took on her mother's maiden name instead of her father's?

Likelihood of success: Worth a shot, at least for the timeline information.

OPTION 2: Meet with *Maître Lancelot.*

I can't speak French to save my life, so tracking him down in Paris would be a little difficult... But if I can get to talk to him in person (he obviously speaks English), I could ask to join that high-class whorehouse so I can have a look for myself. Maybe she'll be there in flesh and blood?

Likelihood of success: Worth a shot.

. . .

OPTION 3: Uncover more information about Ady's wedding.

If I can figure out Gabriella's death information, I could look for Paris weddings that occurred shortly thereafter. Tracking down Ady (or whatever Ady would be short for) could lead me to his ex-girlfriend/my stewardess's name, but seriously... Too many unknowns, and my other two options are more promising.

Likelihood of success: Low to nil.

I've got a bit of research to do before getting on my flight to Paris.

And I'll need some help.

A FRIEND'S HELP

A RARE BOTTLE of Knappogue Castle 1951 whiskey was enough to convince Bob to once again help me track down my mystery stewardess, starting with a real translation of her last entry:

> Nicholas, it's me. Please forget about what I told you last night. I need more time to think about it. I'll call you as soon as I've made my final decision. Very soon I hope.

Yeah for me. Google's translated grammar and sentence structure sucked ass, but I had gotten the gist.

I looked at the large calendar on Bob's home

office wall. Had she taken the job by now? That, I didn't know.

"And what about that obituary I asked you to track down? Anything?" I asked.

"Found something alright, but you've got to spill the beans," he said before typing something on his keyboard, then turning the monitor so I could see it from my side of his desk.

Eight gorgeous, tall, and slender women in colorful bikinis, masks obscuring half of their faces, occupied his large screen. I enjoyed the sight for a few seconds before noticing the elegant woman standing in the center of the group, a fur jacket on and a cigarette holder in her right hand.

"That's her. Right there in the middle of Gorgeousville's finest. Who the fuck was she? Your stewardess? Can we now celebrate the end of your ridiculous quest?"

"No. And I'm so close to finding her. That was her aunt."

His eyebrows went up. "Well, the gene pool certainly seems decent... Even surrounded by those top-notch babes, she still looks attractive. But who are these fine specimens? And what is up with the masks? The article didn't say anything about them. Are they models?"

"Have you checked centerfolds lately?" I asked Bob.

He squinted, as though weighing the odds I was lying to him. "You've got naked pix of them?"

"Fuck, no," I had another look at the big-breasted blonde whose wavy hair flowed down all the way to her tiny waist. "I wish... But there might be a way to get your hands on them for real... if you can afford it."

Bob's eyes widened. "They're whores?"

"That'd be my guess. But high-class ones," I said.

He minimized the image and then returned the monitor to face him. "What the fuck have you gotten yourself into? And how is the dead aunt going to help you find your mystery woman?"

"I was hoping you'd help me find out! Heck, that's what that expensive bottle was for. Tell me you got something."

Bob let out a sigh before turning off his monitor. "All I dug up was that she died a year and a half ago. No cause of death."

I rested my back in my chair. "Did it mention her age?"

"61." Bob got up and walked around his desk. "Now, shall we join Stacy in the dining room?

Dinner's probably ready by now. Don't want to get in trouble for keeping her waiting..."

"Wouldn't have guessed based on that picture," I said, getting up. I followed him out of his office while reflecting on that number. It didn't matter really. The stewardess had mentioned something about being in her early-thirties when she went to Mexico. Assuming her entries were written relatively close to each other, she should be in her mid- or late-thirties at most... Guess I'd be fine with that.

But more than a year has passed since her Paris entry?

A lot *can happen in a year... Including, perhaps, a career change?*

WHAT HAPPENED

WHILE BOB and I were out on his deck digesting the delicious ham dinner Stacy had prepared for us —and smoking a couple of Cuban cigars—I tried to entice him to take a few days off and come to Paris with me to act as my interpreter. But by the time I left that night, I hadn't received an official answer.

That was a week ago, but he finally sent me his answer today via text message:

I'll go, but only if Stacy comes with.

I shook my head as I pressed the button to dial his number. He picked up on the second ring.

"Come on, man!" I said without greeting him. "You really want her to know what we'll be up to?"

"It's my only condition. That, and you're still covering my expenses, as you said you would."

"Why? I like your wife, but this... This is a gentlemen's errand."

"Don't worry," Bob said. "She wants to shop. She'll do her own thing, I swear."

I paused for a second, hoping I'd think of a clever way to convince him. "I can't be held responsible if she sees or hears something she shouldn't."

"What? Are you planning on killing someone?"

"Bob, I don't know how things are between Stacy and you, but let's just say that she could catch you in... a compromising position... or at least in a place that wouldn't be suitable for her."

"You mean we'll go and visit that whorehouse?"

"Possibly."

"Awesome. Don't worry about Stacy. She's cool."

"Fine, let's coordinate our schedules. I'll text you my free dates. Pick those that work for the both of you then."

And this is how and why the three of us ended up traveling to Paris together.

Not according to plan, but I had to roll with the punches.

But wouldn't you know... I got to learn an interesting thing or two I'd have never known—and would have never guessed—about Bob and Stacy while we were in Paris...

Here's how our French adventure unfolded.

WITH THE WI-FI password added to his tablet, Bob began his online search for *Maître Lancelot*. "Sure hope your guy isn't on holiday right now..."

"Doubt his entire office would be closed if that's the case. Someone in his team will help me find her this time."

"Got one here," Bob said as he scrolled down the results page. "Christophe Lancelot."

"Not him. His first name's Nicholas."

He groaned. "And you tell me *now*?"

"Sorry, I thought I'd mentioned it," I said, scanning the room for the nearest waiter.

Seems the staff is in no rush to swing by our table to offer us menus or anything...

"I'll go get us drinks." I got up and headed to the bar. Luckily for me, the waiter spoke English.

Maybe everyone in the French capital speaks it, at least to some extent?

I ordered two beers and returned to the table where Bob sat, his eyes glued to his device.

I handed him a glass. "Here you go."

"Thanks." He took a sip. "Ahhhh. Just what I needed." He took another swig, then rested his drink on the table. "I found two possibilities."

He handed me his tablet and pointed to the open tabs in his browser window. "You know what he looks like?"

I traded my glass for his electronic device, then swiped down the page until I saw a photo of the first Nicholas Lancelot. I couldn't read French, but I spotted his name in one of the captions. The man in question had curly blond hair and a large smile. "Not him." I tapped on the X to close the tab and the other one came into view. Stern, tall, and bald. "That's the one," I said, handing Bob his tablet back. "Can you find out their business hours and address?"

He took another swig, then tapped his way to a different page on their website. "Yup. They should be open tomorrow at 10 a.m. Do you want me to email them, or should I call and see if anyone picks up so I can request an appointment?"

"Doubt they'd be able to book us tomorrow anyway. Why don't we just show up unannounced? Maybe we'll catch him off guard, and he'll divulge something he wouldn't have otherwise?"

He raised his shoulders. "Why not? And I'll make sure Stacy's all set with her shopping plans for the day."

"Now that's a good friend. Hope she won't max out your credit card. Cheers!" I said, clinking my half-empty glass against Bob's.

He shook his head. "I better get my hands on one of those hot babes like you promised."

"No... I'll do everything to try and make it happen. But I never promised *that*."

Bob tilted his head from side to side a few times before taking another swig. "Still worth it. And with your never-ending luck, my odds are probably good."

10:00 A.M.

ARCHITECTURALLY SPEAKING, the facade looked like a regular Parisian residential building. No visible sign that we were at the correct address.

Bob was the first to spot the intercom panel and its multiple buttons in the entranceway, partly hidden behind the glass doors in front of us.

He pulled open the outside door and went in. I followed. I tried the second door, but it was locked.

"Hold on," he said.

I turned and saw him squint at the list of names on the panel. A few seconds later, he pressed a button.

After a minute of waiting, I asked Bob to try

again. "Maybe hold it and speak. See if they can hear you," I said.

He did, and we once again waited for nothing.

But then, just as I was about to give up, a woman unlocked the door from the inside. A young boy was with her. They politely left the door open for us (or I may have squeezed my shoe in the doorway just as it was closing).

Once the woman and her kid were out of sight, I pulled the door opened for Bob to lead the way.

"What floor is it on?" I asked him as we climbed the narrow stairway.

He replied without turning around. "The panel said fourth, but I don't know if it means three or four floors up from here. You know... Ground floor sometimes being first floor and all... Can't remember how French buildings work."

And we could have gotten our answer soon enough, but I didn't care nor keep track of the number of flights we'd climbed before finally seeing the business sign we were looking for.

"Bonjour," a female voice said to us as we stepped in the large lobby. I looked around and saw a young, twenty-something carrot-head behind a desk. Then, after looking at both of us, a long string of incomprehensible blabber spilled out of her mouth, in a tone that was far from the friendliest I'd heard.

Bob took over, seemingly trying to appease the young thing, and I followed him to the reception desk behind which she stood.

That young secretary was cute, in an austere and angry librarian kind of way. Her bright orange hair had been tied into a braid, and she wore glasses with a dark-brown frame that made her skin seem like it'd never been exposed to a single sunbeam. Ever. Her pink lips were bunched as she shook her head at Bob. The line between her brows deepened. She was pointing at the door through which we'd entered.

Shit.

A large brass plate sat on the corner of her desk: *Amélie Desmoines.*

"Amélie," I said, interrupting my friend half-sentence through his French gibberish. "Do you speak English by any chance?"

Her stern face turned to me. "Yes, of course," she said with a thick accent, rolled Rs and all.

"Great. I'm Charlie. I love those glasses, by the way," I said before flashing her my most charming smile.

Her left hand flew to the thick arm of her

eyewear. She blinked a few times, brought up her glasses ever so slightly, then looked at me, this time without that line between her orange brows. Her eyes' shade of brown was so dark, it almost seemed black. *How rare on a redhead. Contacts?*

"Listen. We're so sorry to show up here unannounced... But see, we came all the way from America to see *Maître Lancelot*, and we're only in Paris for a couple of days—"

"That is *not* how it works," she said, shaking her head at me and making her brow line reappear. "You need to book an appointment. *Maître Lancelot* is a very busy man."

"I realize that. And I'm so sorry to inconvenience you." I stepped closer to her, pushing Bob aside, then rested my elbows on the marble surface and leaned toward her. "This is a gorgeous office, by the way. I love the leather furniture, the marble top here," I said, sliding my fingers toward her on the surface that separated us. "Even the staff has that classic look of beauty that never goes out of style."

Her cheeks flushed.

Got her.

"Did you know that my friend and I are airline pilots? I assure you that we can more than cover

any inconvenience caused by our unexpected visit."
I paused and looked at her, gauging what my next
move should be. "Maybe I can take you out to
dinner tonight? Fancy place... Your pick... What do
you say?" I asked.

Her hand flung to her collarbone, and she
played with the tip of her braid.

My trusty pilot card never fails. Today won't be any different.

She squinted at me before replying. "I can't
tonight."

"How's tomorrow night? My last night in
town... My friend Bob here is nice and all, but I
certainly would prefer spending my last night in
Paris in great company..."

She let out a long sigh. "Okay, I'll see what I
can do. Please take a seat," she said, pointing to the
oversized chairs in the waiting area.

A few seconds later, we had both taken a very
comfortable seat out of earshot—at least if we
whispered.

Bob shook his head at me. "What kind of black
magic do you work on women?"

I raised my shoulders. "Natural charm."

"Whatever," he said, picking up a magazine
from the coffee table in front of us.

I looked around the lobby once more. Other than a W.C. door in front of us, there was only one more door, and it was closed. It had to be the lawyer's office.

"Did the website mention any other lawyers working here?" I asked Bob.

"Nope. You better hope your magic works. Do you plan on getting her to spill the beans over a pillow?"

The thought made me smile. "That's not a bad idea... But I don't know if she knows anything about my stewardess." I turned to the reception area. The redhead was on the phone, presumably talking with *Maître Lancelot*.

"Hey," I said, tapping on Bob's magazine to get his attention. "What if I tried to get her to step away from her computer..." I whispered to Bob. "...Long enough for you to go and see if she's got some information about that Gabriella Andrews. There've gotta be some records. Her niece's name and number, an address, something, don't you think?" I sat back in my seat and looked at my friend.

He frowned then leaned toward me. "You realize you're asking me to do something ill—" he mumbled quietly before straightening up and donning a large smile.

I looked up and realized the secretary had walked up to us.

Damned Turkish rug must have silenced the clicks of her stilettos. Quite the legs on that one...

Unfortunately, she forced me to skip my more detailed appraisal of her goods by addressing us too quickly.

"I just got off the phone with *Maître Lancelot*. He cannot make it today, but he said he is willing to spare 15 minutes of his time tomorrow at 11 o'clock. Would that work for you gentlemen?"

"Sure," Bob said as he got up.

Shit. That leaves us with nothing to go on.

"Then, if you'll accompany me, I'll walk you down to the front door and let you out," she said, pointing at that damned door again. "I'll grab my keys, and I'll be right back."

Quick, Charlie. Think of something.

But nothing had come to mind by the time she joined us again.

She asked us to follow her out of the main office door, her purse strapped around her shoulder. I watched her tiny round ass lead us down that narrow staircase. Her short tailored skirt and the back seams on her nylons that lined up perfectly with those pencil heels didn't help me think straight either.

We'd gone down a full flight of stairs when I suddenly stopped and turned around to face Bob, who was following me—thankfully quite a few steps behind.

"Hey, didn't you say you needed to use the bathroom?" I asked Bob with one of my hands directly in front of my chest, wiggling my fingers to mime typing the best I could without Amélie seeing any of it, hoping he'd understand my plan.

He cleared his throat while his eyes sent daggers flying my way. He was shaking his head.

I opened my eyes as big as I could. "Are you sure?"

A second passed before he folded. "Yeah, you're probably right. I don't think I'll be able to make it back to the hotel in time." He moved his head so he could make eye contact with the receptionist a few steps below me. "I saw you had a washroom in there. Would it be alright if I quickly ran back up and used it?"

I turned to watch her reaction and silently prayed.

That line reappeared between her brows. After

letting out a loud sigh, she finally gave him permission. But she also started climbing back up the stairs.

I threw my arm up to block her path, brushing her small breasts in the process.

She frowned at me.

"Amélie," I started while lowering my arm. "Why don't you and I head down and wait for him by the front door? Get some fresh air, get to know each other..."

She shook her head and squeezed next to me as she passed me on the stairs. "No, I left my comp—"

"Okay, I didn't want to embarrass Bob but..."

She stopped, turned around, then looked at me. "But what?"

"He's got a bad case of diarrhea. I'm sure he'd appreciate a little privacy... And you probably wouldn't want to hear the noises that come out of him either."

She rolled her eyes. "Fine. But I need to smoke. You are pushing my limits."

"Fine by me!" I said, bringing my back against the wall to clear her path down. "Lead the way, beautiful."

10:35 A.M.

IT WAS ONLY after we hailed a cab and both slid onto the backseat that Bob lashed out at me.

"Are you fucking out of your mind?" he yelled, his fist tightly wound up and aiming at me, his nostrils flaring.

I raised my hands as though they were a peace barrier between us. "Man, I get it. Not cool at all. I'm sorry." Bob wasn't moving, but I could see him clench his jaw. "Come on. You *had* to take one for the team. I couldn't leave you alone with her. From what I saw, she hates you. Did you get anything?"

He dropped his fist, but I could tell he was still fuming. He kept shaking his head, looking at his feet, his mouth turned upside down.

Shit. He got nothing? How else will I get information then? Pillow talk tomorrow night?

Nah... Not his fault, though.

"Man, don't worry about it. Nothing bad happened; you didn't get caught."

"Nothing? NOTHING?" he repeated, screaming at me, making the cabbie turn and yell something at us in French.

Bob lowered his voice, but his facial expression made it clear he was pissed. Sweat was beginning to pearl on his forehead. "What if they have security cameras? What if I forgot to close a tab. What if—"

"Relax, Bob!" I slapped him on the shoulder. "Hey, look at me!" I waited until I got his full attention. "She's got absolutely NO REASON to even think that you've looked at her computer. I told her you had diarrhea. A bad case of it. Doubt they have a security camera in there. And even if they do, she doesn't know your last name. How many American Bobs do you know? Absolutely no worries, man!"

But my words didn't seem to reach my friend's ears. His entire body was shaking, something I'd never witnessed once since meeting him, decades ago.

"What about fingerprints?" he asked.

"What? Come on! This is real life. Not fucking CSI. Did you steal something while you were in there?"

He swallowed hard while shaking his head rapidly.

"Then there's nothing to worry about. By now, she's back to work, none the wiser. Her own fingers have already covered and smudged whatever print you may have left on her keyboard. NOTHING to worry about, man!"

He was now breathing deeply. Inhaling and exhaling while moving his hands up and down in front of him.

"Okay. Okay," he said.

"Sorry. I promise I won't ask you to do anything like that again. Drinks on me."

He exhaled loudly, wiped his forehead, then dug his phone out of his pant pocket. "You're right. I'm freaking out for nothing. She's got nothing on me."

I watched him unlocked his screen and I finally relaxed a bit.

Fuck. No idea Bob could turn into such a nervous wreck.

"So, you want to see what I found?" he asked.

I GRABBED MY PHONE, then opened my navigation app to enter the address shown in the photo Bob had taken of Gabriella's business data sheet.

Sure, he hadn't found anything about her niece, but an address could be useful... Assuming it was what I hoped it was.

After pressing the *Search* button, I crossed my fingers and waited.

And there it was: a large acreage within driving distance from here.

"Fuck yes!" I said. I wrapped my arm around Bob's shoulders. "You did it, man! This is the place!"

"What place?"

I looked toward the cabbie and my eyes met his in the rearview mirror.

"I'll tell you as soon as we sit ourselves in that hotel bar. You're gonna like this." After the freak-out Bob had just put me through. I simply couldn't believe it. "You're the man," I said, feeling a smile grow on my face.

I FILLED Bob in on the details I knew as soon as we got ourselves a couple of cold ones.

"But if there's a gate, and you have to say your name to get past it, what the fuck is your plan?" he asked.

"Well... We can wear mask to hide who we are... but you got a point." I stared at the condensation that started to drip down my bottle. "I have no freaking idea, unless you're willing to shave your head and pretend to be that lawyer? That's the only name I know, and I don't know how tall the fucker is, so... I don't have a plan."

Shit. Why did I get my hopes up so fast?

"Do you think we could somehow climb over

the fence without having to give our names?" Bob asked.

I thought about it for a second. "No idea. Maybe, but there's a guy at the front door who does valet parking. Showing up without a car would be strange."

Bob took a swig, and so did I.

"Is there a side door we could use?" he asked.

"Shit, I think they have cameras outside. And they definitely do inside."

Bob waved his hand in the air. "So all of this stress for nothing? Really?"

"What do you suggest?" I asked. "We attach ourselves to another vehicle that's going in? Right under the axle, James Bond style? Then somehow distract the driver and sneak our way in? Don't think that would be good for your stress level..."

We finished our beers in silence and ordered another round.

An idea sparked in my head the moment the cold liquid of the next beer hit my mouth. "We don't get in. We wait until one of them gets out, then we follow her."

Bob furrowed his brow. "Her who? Your mystery woman?"

"That would be fantastic, but unlikely. We

follow one of the whores, then question her once she's out of the brothel."

"We stalk her?" He took another sip, seemingly pondering the idea. "What time do they finish working?"

"No idea."

"And what if it's a live-in brothel?"

"From what I read, it seems they only offer *evening services*. The ladies must go home at some point..."

"So, we're going to follow some random beautiful woman back home?"

I tilted my head while bringing the bottle to my lips again.

It could possibly get us in trouble... But let's hope my lucky star stays on my side a bit longer.

"That's the plan, unless you have a better idea," I said.

"And it could be one of the gorgeous girls in that photo with the dead woman?"

"Possibly," I said, my shoulders raising on their own.

"Well... The risk would be worth it then... I'll need to take a nap this afternoon if we're going to spend the night staring at a gate."

"And I guess I'll go rent us a car. A cab won't do for tonight."

I finished my beer, then took out my wallet. After retrieving a few bills, I flagged our waiter over. Bob too was done and getting up from his chair.

"Meet down here at 8," I told him. "And wear something nice. We don't want her to think we're regular creeps. I'll go buy some binoculars, too. They could be handy."

"I WONDER how much this one costs..." Bob said, his eyes glued to the binoculars.

I poured myself another cup of coffee from the Thermos we'd brought. Even with the overhead light near the security camera, I couldn't see much without binoculars. Bob had parked too far for that, but any closer would have been suspicious. "What is it?" I asked.

"Mercedes. Convertible."

"Probably a small fortune... like a membership to this whorehouse."

He lowered his binoculars and looked at me. "Mercedes, MG, Rolls-Royce, Maserati... Everyone here's loaded."

I sipped the hot liquid, letting it warm my throat and help keep my eyes open. "We're not poor ourselves," I reminded Bob.

"No. But I don't spend frivolously on cars..."

I muffled a laugh. "Cause Stacy gets to your money first," I said.

He laughed. "Yeah. She's a big spender."

Another vehicle had turned onto our deserted street. Its lights first pointing toward us, then toward the metal gate when it turned into the entrance. Bob brought his binoculars up again.

"HEY, remember when I stayed at your place in Costa Rica?" I asked.

"Yeah?" Bob nodded.

"I forgot to ask you. Henrietta, who is she?"

"You saw her?" He dropped his binoculars and looked at me. "What did you think?"

"I saw a woman, but I don't know if it was Henrietta. You didn't tell me anything about her."

"She could compete with those brothel ladies in terms of looks, but maybe a bit rounder..."

"Would she swim naked in the pool?"

"Ah! That's the one. You did her, you dog?"

"No, I didn't even talk to her. But what's her deal?"

"Let's just say that she spices up my Costa Rican getaways."

I watched yet another car turn into the entrance. "With Stacy there?"

He let out a long sigh. "We have an arrangement. We've been married so long..."

I frowned and looked at him, unsure if I'd misheard.

"Remember when things weren't great between me and Stacy? A while back?"

I nodded. Of course I did. His *dog house* had been my couch for a few weeks.

"We met with a therapist, and turns out we both craved more variety. So we quit going to that overqualified bitch and started seeing other people instead. Henrietta is my other person in Costa Rica."

"But how can you have an affair with her when Stacy's right there with you? That complex isn't that big."

"No, not an affair. Stacy knows about her. She knows Henrietta *very well*."

"What the..." I stared at my friend in the dim moonlight. No spark in his eyes. No hint of a smile. *He's serious.* "Well, hats off to you... And to Stacy." And then I had my light bulb moment. "Ahhhh!

That's why you thought Stacy wouldn't be in the way if she came with us to Paris? Did you tell her what we're up to tonight?"

He raised his left hand. "Whoa! She doesn't know—or need to know—everything. She's got no clue about your obsession with this mystery stewardess. I told her we were going to a *special establishment*, and that maybe I'd bring back some late-night entertainment for us."

The words that came out of Bob's mouth were blowing my fucking mind.

"You have trios with your wife?" I asked.

He nodded and smiled. "Yeah. I still love her. She's hot. And that way we can add variety without the guilt, shame, and paranoia that come with cheating."

I realized my head had been shaking. Unsure for how long, though.

Incredible.

"But, your wife is into other women... or... Do you..." My hands started moving as though they could express what I wasn't going to say aloud.

"Do we sometimes have the *Devil's three way*?"

"Yeah. That." I swallowed hard.

"She deserves variety, too," Bob said.

No, he didn't! Shit just got weird.

I could no longer move or speak. I didn't want to ask nor know if there was any touching between him and the other men with whom he shared his wife. And then, just when my discomfort had seemingly reached its apex, memories of that amazing blow job under the table in Ireland flashed back in my mind... A homophobic shiver traversed my body. *The best blow job I've ever gotten.*

"Come on, man. Nothing weird there, I swear." He chuckled. "If you want bizarro, here's something: a couple of years ago, Stacy suggested we add *you* to one of our 'variety evenings'." He punched me on the shoulder. "I like you, man. But that's where I drew the line. *That* would have been fucking weird."

My stare froze somewhere in the darkness in front of the car. Stacy looked like Jennifer Aniston, but even hotter. The Bro Code had always kept her out of bounds, so discovering this little bit of information was weird indeed. "Yeah," I said, nodding.

"But don't tell her I told you—or anyone for that matter. The only reason our arrangement works is because we keep it a secret from the world... And because we respect and love each other. The other people are just a means to an end. Purely physical. That's it."

I swallowed hard and forced myself out of my stupor.

Am I that old-fashioned?

I started nodding. "Your secret's safe with me."

"Thanks. Appreciate it. So, are you gonna become a member of this place?" Bob asked.

"I'll for sure attempt to tomorrow." I looked at my watch. It was already past midnight. "Who knows when we'll get home. I'll have to set up a couple of back-up alarms. But then again, we'll have a car."

"We? Am I going with you again?"

I turned to look at Bob. "I assumed you would, but the lawyer speaks English. And that receptionist really didn't like your face or something."

"Yeah... It's hit and miss with me and women."

1:30 A.M.

A STRING of twenty cars had trickled out of the gates over the past hour.

Our Thermos long empty, my caffeine levels were beginning to dwindle, but I knew our luck was about to turn. If men were leaving, the girls were also likely to start heading home soon.

"Here's another one," I said to Bob.

I waited until the perfect spot where the beams from the car's lights were blocked by the nearby bushes and where the light from the security camera shone directly into the car, illuminating the silhouette of the driver. I saw a ponytail with a long, delicate neck.

"It's a woman," I said. "Finally!"

The boring surveillance task was coming to an end.

"Are we stopping her right here?" Bob asked.

"That would be creepy. Let's follow her and see. Maybe she'll stop at a gas station or something."

"And *that* wouldn't be creepy?" Bob started the engine, letting his rhetorical question die unanswered.

ABOUT FORTY-FIVE MINUTES LATER, she stopped and parallel parked her small Renault, leaving us too close to noticeably do the same without her seeing us.

"What now?" Bob asked as he slowed down.

"Keep driving and go around the block," I said.

We passed her vehicle as she finished backing into her spot. Her head was looking behind her so I couldn't see her face but it was clear her hair was long and blonde.

By the time we came around again, she was nowhere to be seen, but another parking spot was available nearby.

"Park here," I ordered Bob.

He did.

"Now what? Unless you saw something I missed earlier, we've lost her. Smart move, Charlie," Bob said with a smirk after turning off the engine.

I leaned forward and looked out of the windshield. Very few windows had their lights turned on. Most of the people in the neighborhood appeared to be fast asleep.

"Either she lives around here, or she went for a night cap some place. Can you think of another reason why she'd have parked here?"

"You want to start buzzing doorbells and asking around? At this time of night?" Bob asked.

"Of course not! But do you think you'd be able to get straight home after a night doing what she does? I'm going for a walk. Come on."

We exited the vehicle and Bob locked it, its single but loud beep probably annoying a few insomniacs and waking up others. Then we started walking down the deserted streets of Paris. But at least we were doing it in style with our dark suits, although quite a bit wrinkled from a night spent sitting in the car.

The first street was nothing but residential, save for a few shops on the ground level, all with their metal doors rolled down to the ground and locked.

We continued our walk around the block, heading back to our starting point when I saw a small neon sign on a street corner one block away. I recognized one of the beer brands we'd been drinking.

"There?" I asked Bob.

"Fine. You're buying," he said, not bothering to hide a yawn.

Why are yawns contagious? I followed suit then rubbed my face in an effort to wake up a bit.

Two minutes later, we walked into the establishment, which was near empty.

No blonde ponytailed lady anywhere.

"Shit," I muttered under my breath, but Bob headed to an empty table anyway.

"*Deux bière*s," I said to the bartender, practicing what Bob had been teaching me earlier tonight. When he looked back at me with a question I didn't understand, I turned to Bob who replied, "Amstel."

Damn language barrier.

The bartender uncapped our bottles and placed them on top of the bar while I dug out my wallet. I handed him a twenty-euro bill. He finished ringing our order in his till and was handing me my change when a high-pitch voice made me turn my head.

And there she was. The ponytailed whore.

Certainly didn't look like one, though. She looked like a super-model who'd rolled out of bed and put on sweats. Big blue eyes. Blonde hair that glistened and sparkled even in the crappy lighting of this beat-up bar. I elbowed Bob.

He looked at me. "No idea how your ass can hold so much luck. Every fucking time," he said.

I handed him the two brand-new beers. "Offer her a drink and chat her up. Find out about where she works. Try to get the name of her new boss..."

3:15 A.M.

I WASTED an hour of my time sitting at the bar, watching my friend make progress with the gorgeous lady. Between a couple of beers, a bottle of carbonated water, and a pack of nuts, I had run out of diversions. My patience—and my wakefulness—was wearing thin, so I decided to check up on him.

I walked over to the table and leaned close to him.

"Got something," he whispered to me. "I'll try and get more."

"I'll head home. Lucky night for you," I said in his ear. Then I straightened up and spoke louder. "You'll find your way home?"

He handed me the car keys, then gave me the thumbs up. I walked away, but just as I pushed open the front door, I turned back to my friend whose arm was wrapped around the blonde's shoulders. "Leave me a note under my door if you make it back before my appointment."

The air was crisp and cool, like a mild slap in the face that awakened me enough to safely make it back to the hotel.

"COFFEE WOULD BE FANTASTIC," I said.

For a second I wondered if I could somehow sneak a peek at Amélie's monitor while she was preparing it, but no luck. The machine was just behind her reception desk.

Damn it.

My hand went to my pant pocket, and I felt the paper note Bob had slid under my door. The only word on it was 'Sophia.'

Is it my stewardess's name? Or maybe just last night's whore's name...

He hadn't picked up my call earlier, but I could clarify it later today when I saw him.

I returned my attention to Amélie. She was

standing in front of the chromed coffee machine, pressing buttons that chimed loudly.

"Are you still taking me out tonight?" she asked with a smile.

She seemed in a much better mood today than yesterday. In fact, that annoying line between her brows had yet to appear, and she'd been smiling at me the entire time since I'd gotten here today.

"Of course. I'm a man of my word." I replied, admiring her slender figure. *Stilettos again today.*

And just then, she gave me a sly smile before stretching her arm up to adjust the position of the picture frame that hung above the coffee machine. In doing so, she exposed the lacy edge of her pantyhose where her skirt ended. *Ooh la la.* She definitely wasn't wearing those ass-covering granny hoses, and her small ass was too tightly wrapped in that fabric to hide suspenders...

And then, her arm was back down, but she didn't bother to pull down her skirt. With a clink, she placed my small coffee cup on a silver tray and came toward me.

"I saw you looking at me," she said with a wink.

I raised my right hand and smiled. "Guilty as charged. You're beautiful. It's hard *not* to look at you."

"Well, if you play your cards right, maybe I'll let you look at every—"

"Charlie?" a deep man's voice asked two feet away from me on my right.

I turned and recognized the bald lawyer I'd seen on the website. I shook his hand. "Thanks for seeing me on such short notice."

"No problem, but I only have fifteen minutes. I'm Nicholas by the way. Shall we go into my office? Amélie will bring in your coffee." He turned his attention to the receptionist. "And can you please make another one for me as well?"

I followed the man into his office, which was as impressive as my stewardess had described it. Amélie was following me, tray in hand, which she placed on the large desk in front of me, then transferred the saucer and cup to the lacquered wood surface before walking out, blurting something in French to Nicholas as she did. He replied to her in French, then turned his attention to me.

"So, why did you want to talk to me so urgently?" he asked.

I dove right in, taking full advantage of my limited time slot. "I'm here because of Gabriella Andrews and her business."

Although his poker face was pretty good, something flashed in his eyes when I mentioned her name. He stayed quiet for a solid minute. Then, he finally spoke. "I'm not following you, Charlie. Why are you here, and why are you talking to me about this woman?"

Amélie walked in with his coffee and I held off replying until she left the room.

"Please close the door on your way out," he said, in English this time.

"Oh, please cut the crap. I know she's dead. I know you two were close, and I know you were taking care of her business's legal issues. I'm not here to give you any trouble. Far from it. In fact, I'd like to apply to become a member, if it's at all possible."

He leaned back in his chair for a few seconds. "And where did you acquire this alleged information?"

"Listen, Nicholas. I know the entire business is on the gray side of things, and I'm not planning on running to the authorities with what I know. I just want to join. It's not like you have a public website, do you? I have no idea how the application process works. But I know you're involved, so I'm hoping you can tell me how to do it. Who took over after Ms. Andrews died?"

"I'm not at liberty to say anything to you. Our office doesn't represent any businesses that offer illegal services." He got up from his chair. "I'm going to ask you to leave now. I'm afraid I can't help you."

"And what about Sophia? Can you give me her contact information?"

He frowned at me, his nostrils flaring as he exhaled loudly.

I've clearly overstayed my welcome or trespassed some invisible boundary.

"Come on," I said. "Let me at least leave a business card with you. If you change your mind, you'll know where to contact me so I can send my money to become a member." I dug my wallet out and then handed him a card.

Unexpectedly, he took it and had a glance at it. "You're a pilot for a US-based airline? You don't even live here..."

"But I fly into Charles-de-Gaulle fairly regularly. I'd be willing to pay full price to access this particular business a few times per month. Think about it."

He let out yet another sigh then tossed my card into his waste basket.

What an ass.

Having never been a sore loser, I put on a fake smile and held out my hand. "Thank you for your time."

He shook my hand, then I turned around and let myself out of his office.

"That was fast," Amélie said. "You'll pick me up here?"

"Sure. What time are you off?"

"19... No, how do you say...?" she started before looking up. "7 p.m.," she said.

"I'll be here, just outside your front door. I'll let you make the reservation to your favorite place. But just so I dress the part, are we going to a casual or fancy restaurant?"

She tilted her head and winked at me. "Fancy. Let me walk you out," she said before grabbing her set of keys and leading me down the narrow staircase.

AS PROMISED, my redhead left her office at 7 p.m. sharp.

Punctuality from a woman always surprised me. If she kept that simple promise, how would her promise to expose more of herself pan out? She'd for sure deliver on that, right?

With her looking left and right on the sidewalk across the street, I got that she hadn't spotted me yet. "Amélie!" I called out, waving at her.

She turned my way, her hand went up, and then she nodded.

I'd snatched a great parking spot just across the street from her office, but I was pretty sure that the blue and red circle meant I'd parked illegally, so I wanted to stay nearby, ready to move the car at a second's notice if needed. She crossed the busy street in the same outfit I'd seen her wear in this morning: an off-white blouse with her short black skirt... and those sheer stockings and fabulous stilettos.

A vision of her bare body wearing nothing but those heels flashed in my mind. But the sudden squealing of car brakes made the thought disappear before it'd reached my groin.

She slapped the guilty car's hood and yelled what I could only assume were some French insults at the male driver who snapped something back at her.

My inner gentleman felt a tad guilty for not having helped her cross traffic, but then again, she was a grown woman. And one with quite a character it seemed...

Finally off the street, she traded her frown for a large smile then leaned into me to kiss me once on each cheek. She smelled of pears and peaches.

"Shall we get going?" I asked.

She nodded and I led her to the passenger door of my car and opened it for her once the traffic allowed me to.

She climbed in. I watched her lean legs fold into

her seated position, the top of her stockings once again visible and enticing. She placed her purse on her lap, and I closed her door before making my way around the car to the driver's seat.

"So where to?" I asked her after doing up my seat belt and starting the engine.

"Well... After the dream I had last night, I think there's only one option that will satisfy me."

"What dream?" I asked. *Women's brains made it impossible to converse in a straight line.*

Her hands left her purse and launched for my right thigh. "Let's just say you played a part in it... An important part," she said, one of her hands locked on my knee while the other slowly slid up my thigh. Then she let go of my leg just as quickly as she'd reached for it. She dug a piece of paper out of her purse and handed it to me.

"What do you think of this menu?" she asked.

Stuck in traffic that wasn't going anywhere, I had a look. The cursive hand-writing read as follows:

Chez Amélie

Entrée ~ Ma chatte carotte

Plat principal ~ Ton saucisson américain

Dessert ~ Fricassé de jambes en l'air

"You know I don't speak *any* French, right?" I asked her, confused. But the title told me she wanted to go to her place. Then I spotted the word *dessert*. It had to be the menu she wanted to cook at home?

Her smile grew higher on one side of her face. Then she winked and returned one of her hands to my thigh. "I'll teach you a few words then. Drive. I'll tell you where to turn."

MY CAR PARKED, I followed her into a residential building.

We climbed a long staircase in silence, and I enjoyed every step of it, my eyes locked onto Amélie's gorgeous, tiny ass in front of me. The lines on the back of her legs sometimes distracted me from her swaying hips as she climbed, but I resisted the urge to flat out grab her—unsure why, though. It was becoming clearer and clearer that she and I shared the same goal.

Why else would a beautiful woman bring home a near stranger when I've clearly offered to put on pretenses and take her out to dinner?

Once she reached the landing for her floor, she

veered toward one of the two doors and dug her keys out of her purse. A few loud clunky turns through the keyhole later, she opened her door for me.

I walked in. Other than the little bit of light that came in from the stairway, it was pitch black.

A second later, she turned on the light and pushed the door closed behind us. Then I followed her past the entrance.

I don't know what I expected exactly—perhaps a modern apartment filled with IKEA furniture or a traditional old-fashioned room with turn-of-the-century furnishings—but what occupied the room was neither. Other than a coat rack and small table where she'd just dropped her keys and purse and a mini kitchen in the far corner with two bar stools that stood below a raised counter, the apartment was bare, the blinds fully down, two other doors closed. The only other *furniture* I could see dangled from the ceiling, dead center in the room: a wide and curvy metal bar with a bunch of suspended straps and stirrups attached to it, some padded, some not. Straight below it, a pile of cushions in assorted colors.

"*Bienvenue chez moi,*" she said. "Can I hang your jacket?"

I took it off and handed it to her.

After hanging it on the rack by the door, she headed straight for the contraption. She grabbed a hold of the straps, then hopped on and sat on the wide, padded one, then her feet found homes in the stirrups.

I loosened my tie and undid my top shirt button as I walked closer to her.

"First course on tonight's menu..." she started, waiting for me to make eye contact with her. "*Ma chatte*. Here's your first lesson," she said before parting her legs. Her mini skirt rode up as her trimmed red bush greeted me.

I walked to her. For a country that invented French-kissing, you'd think they'd do a bit more foreplay before getting to the point, but her pussy sounded deliciously fine to me.

"How about I get you naked first?" I asked as I positioned myself between her legs. My fingers headed toward the delicate ivory buttons of her blouse. One by one, I undid them, exposing a spaghetti-strapped, embroidered, skin-colored slip that continued under her skirt.

She tightened her legs around mine and let go of the straps before slipping out of her unbuttoned blouse and tossing it on the floor. She returned her hands to the straps of the swing and released her thigh clasp.

I reached behind the small of her back and found the zipper of her skirt. I undid it, and as a good and helpful girl, she pushed away from me, hopped out of her seated position, and then stood up. Deliciously slowly, she shimmied out of her mini-skirt before stepping out of it, letting one of her stilettos kick the unwanted item away.

Now wearing nothing but her short slip, sexy stockings, and stilettos, she stared me in the eyes, then hopped back onto the padded strap of her swing, this time resting her thighs on it and letting her ass hang behind it.

I slid my fingers between the silky fabric and her soft, white skin. I slowly made my way up her upper body, all the while placing myself between her legs and bringing her up, letting her weight rest on my thighs, her own thighs wrapped around my legs and allowing her to let go of the straps while I finally got that slip over her head.

I stepped back and watched her swing naked in front of me.

She was beautiful. The whitest of any skin tone I'd ever seen, almost blueish. The thick parts of her sheer stocking contrasted against her legs like two black piano keys. The pink nipples that crowned her small, perky breasts pointed to the ceiling.

I walked back toward her and stopped her swinging motions. I reached behind her head and my fingers found a long pin in her hair. I pulled it out and tossed it.

She shook her head, letting her long orange hair flow, and her fruity smell envelop me in the process. Her dark eyes met mine. A hand behind her delicate neck, I finally allowed myself to taste her pink lips.

Hungry wasn't strong enough of a word to describe her behavior. Famished was more like it. After nearly sucking my soul out of my mouth, she pushed me away. "Eat my pussy," she ordered.

"With pleasure," I said, kneeling on the silky cushions.

My head was at the perfect height. The sight was incredible. The smell was mysterious, musky, and inviting.

I wrapped my hands around her ankles and quickly brushed my way up her thin legs until I reached the thick band holding her stockings in place. Then I slowed to a crawl, titillating each inch of her soft, white flesh up to the fold of her legs and her red carpet. With my index finger, I traced an X through her trimmed bush, then I started brushing three fingers up and down her inviting pink pussy. I let the tip of my middle finger go in and gauge her readiness. It was unnecessary, though, since she was dripping wet. I brought my finger to my lips and licked off her juices. She tasted of a misty autumn morning by the sea.

She adjusted her position on her swing, somehow becoming horizontal in front of me; the strap she was previously sitting on now split into two, one supporting her shoulders and the other supporting her lower back. I could now open her legs as wide as I wanted, so I crammed myself as close as possible to her private, red-thatch-roofed pleasure center.

Hungry for her glistening pussy, I dove in head first.

With one hand, I squeezed her ass while my tongue tickled her small folds. I let her moans guide my mouth. I explored every bit of her pussy and tongue-fucked her while my cock wanted nothing more than a piece of the action. I tickled her. I licked her. I bit her. My tongue poked at her while my fingers rubbed her nub. She was so wet, like a flowing fountain of pussy juice. Her loud moans echoed against the unfurnished walls. I parted her folds then inserted two of my fingers inside her. I let them do what my cock desperately wanted to do to her swollen pussy. Then her thighs squeezed my head as she came in record-time. I swear she squirted in my mouth, and I enjoyed dining on her musky, salty juices. She finally yelled out something in French before releasing my head of her thigh grasp.

She sat back up in her swing and put two fingers under my chin.

"Your turn," she said. "Get up and strip for me."

I did. But with my cock ready to pounce, let's just say that I opted for efficiency instead of seduction.

"Now come and stand right here," she said, pointing to a purple cushion on the floor.

I obeyed and she repositioned herself on her swing. She first swung the device around 180 degrees, then stepped into the stretchy leg stirrups and brought them up around her legs, past her knees and up to the lower part of her thighs. Then she moved the two padded straps she'd previously used behind her back so they now crossed her hips and shoulders. Facing down, she leaned forward until she was parallel to the front. Her legs supported in the stirrups; her hips and shoulders supported by the straps; her small breasts left to hang loose, her arms free to roam wherever they wished.

And my ass is what they went for.

For a split second, I was afraid my cock would poke her in the eyes as she pulled herself toward me, but with a quick flick of her wrist, she re-aimed my erection straight into her wide-open mouth.

"God!" I said as she swallowed half of me.

I put my hands on her shoulders and pulled then pushed her entire body in front of me, as if she were a weightless super-woman giving me head mid-flight. Her warm mouth felt heavenly, her tongue twirled around my shaft. Amélie, in nothing but her lined stockings and stilettos, was quickly making me reach my point of no return. I reached for her firm butt but heard her gag reflex as my cock hit the back of her throat. Instead I reached under her and massaged her breasts as she delighted me with her tongue. Within seconds, I was done for. I exploded in her mouth, then felt the warmth of my own jism dripping on the top of my feet.

She leaned back and returned to a standing position. She stuck out her devilish tongue and licked her lower lip and chin, which glimmered from my cum.

Looking at me, she asked, "Water?"

"Sure. I'd love some," I said, my heart still pounding in my chest.

She made her way to her small fridge, opened the door, then walked back toward me with two small Perrier bottles.

Now, I know nothing about product marketing, but if someone had recorded a video of her walking toward me naked like she did, with so much hedonistic hunger in her eyes, her pussy swollen with desire, and two bottles of Perrier in hand... I'd have instantly gone and bought a truckload of this shit (or at least a whole lot of Perrier shares).

"Drink up," she ordered as her fingers grazed my abs. "I'll need you for another round shortly."

I watched her quench her thirst, debating whether I should ask her about Sophia.

Maybe I could lie my way to the truth?

"Wanna hear how I found your office?" I asked Amélie between two sips.

She raised her shoulders while downing the rest of her bottle.

"A friend of mine is a client of yours. An American woman called Sophia," I said.

She stared me down. "Sophia?" she repeated, slowly.

"Yes. Do you know her?"

She tilted her head. "Is this why you're here?" she asked me, her eyes now two thin slits.

A red alarm sounded in my head.

Shit. Bringing up another woman probably doesn't qualify as good fucking etiquette.

"No, of course not. I'm here for you, gorgeous Amélie." I moved closer and wrapped my arms around her waist.

She snaked her way out of my embrace. "Nicholas warned me about you, but I didn't want to believe him. You're on some information quest and I'm not going to play your little game. Get out!" she yelled, pointing at the door.

"I swear this isn't it. I'm here for you, baby!"

"Don't baby me! Get dressed and get out!"

The temper she'd displayed with Bob had resurfaced, now aimed at me.

Guess that meant round two wasn't going to happen.

NEXT STEPS

SOPHIA...

My instincts—or just hopeful thoughts?—told me she was my stewardess, now turned pimp-mistress, or whatever her official title was.

Now what? Will Nicholas reconsider my request for membership and contact me?

I doubt it. I don't think he liked me very much. Or maybe he doesn't like Americans in general?

But who cares. No point wasting my time thinking about him.

Gotta focus on what I can control...

And a trip to the Netherlands sounds like a fun experience to duplicate, hopefully with a woman as open-minded as my mysterious stewardess. And I may just find another clue that will bring me closer to her.

Sophia...

That's not enough for me to find her, but a first name is something.

Or maybe she spells it Sofia? She does speak Spanish after all... And French.

Damn, could she be smarter than me?

Nah, probably not.

I know I'll outwit her very soon in our cat and mouse game.

TO BE CONTINUED...

...IN PART 8 of *The Stewardess's Diary*, available at most major book retailers.

The complete episodic novel is also available in one (thick) paperback with exclusive author's notes about the series and what inspired each episode.

ABOUT THE AUTHOR

S.M. Pratt is a single woman traveling the world on her own, living in the moment, looking for more than love, and always trying out new things. Fun adventures and unique cultural experiences are always at the top of her agenda, no matter the country she happens to be visiting.

She would love to quit her day job and write full-time. You can help her write the next story faster by purchasing her books and/or giving her five-star reviews. Without your support, she's invisible and unable to make a living doing what she loves, which is creating what you love to read.

If you haven't done so already, please join her private reader group for previews, exclusive offers, and more. It's free: https://smpratt.com

For more information:
smpratt.com
info@smpratt.com